Chogan and the Winnebago Merchant
Book #4 in the Chogan Native American Series

By

Larry Buege

Gastropod Publishing
Marquette, Michigan

Other books by Larry Buege

Miracle In Cade County (Mystery/Love Story)
Cold Turkey (Political Satire)
Bear Creek (Humorous)
Super Mensa (Techno-Thriller)
William Goodman: Civil War Horsesoldier

Native American Novels

Chogan and the Gray Wolf
Chogan and the White Feather
Chogan and the Sioux Warrior

Published by Gastropod Publishing, Marquette, Michigan
Copyright © 2019 by Larry Buege

Library of Congress Control Number: 2019901971
ISBN: 978-0-9892477-8-8

Native American Series

Chogan and the Winnebago Merchant is the fourth novel in the Chogan Native American Series. If you enjoy *Chogan and the Winnebago Merchant* you will probably enjoy the other *Chogan novels. Beware: If you are not careful, you may learn about America's Native American heritage.*

Ojibway Words

Chogan and the Winnebago Merchant uses several Ojibway words, which may confuse some readers. To make the novel more enjoyable, their English translations are listed below. The Ojibway Indians spoke a variation of the Algonquian language, one of the most widely used Native American languages in North America. None of the Indians north of Mexico had a written language; therefore, all spellings are European interpretations and have many variations. Spellings for Chogan's tribe include: Ojibway, Ojibwe, Ojibwa, Ojibubway, Otchipwe, and Chippewa. Americans are more likely to use Chippewa, whereas Canadians prefer Ojibway. Ojibway is an exonym or word used by neighboring tribes and refers to the puckering of Ojibway moccasins. The Ojibway refer to themselves as Anishinabe.

1. Chogan (blackbird)
2. Kanti (sings)
3. Gitche Gumee (Lake Superior or large lake)
4. Hassun (stone)
5. Wagosh Lake (fox)
6. wapatoo (duck potato plant)
7. Takoda (friend to everyone—Sioux)
8. Nawkaw (wood in Winnebago)
9. Kitchi-miniss (Grand Island)
10. Giwaydin Ahnung (North Star)
11. Baggataway (ball game, now called lacrosse)
12. Tatanka (bison or buffalo)
13. Wambleeska (White Eagle—Sioux)

Chapter One

"Chogan, wake up."

The blunt end of Kanti's spear probed my ribs to emphasize her point. She was never one for subtleties. I pushed the spear aside, but it quickly found a new rib. I reluctantly opened my eyes.

"Kanti, it is still dark. Go back to bed." I rolled toward the wigwam wall, hoping Kanti would take the hint—she would not. She continued prodding me with her spear.

"We need to talk," Kanti whispered, "outside."

She obviously didn't want to wake Mother or Grandfather. What she had to say was for my ears only. I should have felt honored, but I didn't.

Grandfather moved into our wigwam after Father died from the fever. I could hear him and Mother breathing deeply. There was little chance of waking them, but Kanti wasn't poking them with the blunt end of her spear.

"This better be good," I replied.

I reluctantly pushed myself away from my sleeping bench along the wigwam wall and staggered toward the door. Kanti was holding the door flap up to offer encouragement. I was still half asleep and needed every bit of encouragement; however, the cold, pre-dawn air quickly revived me. Robins were cheerfully chirping, suggesting the sun might soon make an appearance. I didn't know why robins insisted upon being cheerful. If they wished to awaken before dawn, they could at least be quiet about it. When left to my own schedule I seldom saw a sunrise.

"Something terrible is about to happen."

Now that I was fully awake I could see Kanti was trembling. Her voice quivered as she spoke. Whatever was bothering her was real—at least to her. I looked around. The sky was clear and filled with stars, although they were beginning to fade with the coming dawn. There was no sight of a pending storm. There was nothing to suggest a herd of maladjusted moose were bearing down on our small village. I could find nothing ominous that needed my immediate attention this early in the morning.

"What is this terrible event that must intrude upon my sleep?" I hoped Kanti appreciated my sarcasm.

"I had this dreadful dream where I fell into a hole—like a rabbit hole. There was total darkness, and I could only crawl forward. I couldn't turn around and go back. I heard a moaning sound in front of me. It sounded like death. Then I got stuck in the tunnel. Chogan, you have never seen such darkness."

"It was a dream, Kanti. Dreams can be scary, but they can't hurt you."

"What if this dream comes true?" Kanti asked. "I don't want to die, not alone in such darkness."

"Kanti, you are skinny but still too fat to fall into a rabbit hole."

I had seen twelve winters, two more than Kanti. I should have felt more compassionate toward my sister, and I would have if it had been daytime. I was not fully aroused and my patience was wearing thin.

"The stars are beginning to fade from the sky," I said, "and the robins are convinced it is almost dawn. Perhaps we can stay up and get an early start on checking our snares." It was unlikely that I could return to sleep now that Kanti had dragged me into the cold air. I might as well make the best of it.

Every boy in our village ran a trap line. I had thirty-two snares that I checked every other day. I caught mostly rabbits, ducks, muskrats, and an occasional beaver. We never caught anything big, but a beaver or a couple of rabbits put meat on our plates. I did have the distinction of being the only boy in the village who needed help from his sister. I receive a lot of ribbing for that.

Kanti is also the only girl in our village who carries a spear. I don't know why she can't enjoy weaving baskets like normal girls. At one time the spear had been mine. Grandfather helped me make it. Its tip was made of sharpened bone. Kanti has since added an eagle feather. I gave the spear to Kanti after Grandfather gave me his special bow. The grip on the bow was covered with fur from a shaggy deer Grandfather shot when he visited the land with no trees. He said the shaggy deer were so plentiful that they sometimes covered the land as far as one could see. He described purple hills that reached up to kiss the sky. If it had been anyone other than Grandfather I would not have believed him. Someday I will travel to the land with no trees and climb those purple hills.

"Good morning," Mother said as she exited our wigwam. "You two are up early."

"We wanted to get an early start on our trap line," I replied. I didn't mention the rabbit hole. I was now fully awake and more compassionate; I didn't want to embarrass Kanti.

"Let me make breakfast while you and Kanti find some firewood." Mother fanned the smoldering coals to life and added some wood. By the time Kanti and I returned with armloads of firewood, mother had steaming bowls of wild rice waiting for us. We dropped the wood next to the fire pit.

"Where's Grandfather?" I asked. The deerskin flap that normally covered the door to the wigwam was tied back revealing Grandfather's empty sleeping bench.

"He's meeting with the village elders," Mother replied. "Word has it the Winnebago traders will soon arrive and many people will gather at our village."

"Will Grandfather be traveling to the village on the far end of the lake?" I asked.

Our village lies on the southern shore of Gitche Gumee, a lake so large it has no distant shore. We were as far east as the Winnebago traders traveled. Sometimes Grandfather traded string and rope made from tree bark for obsidian and pipestone from the land with no trees. Grandfather then traded the stones for corn from the village at the east end of the lake. Corn was a welcome change from wild rice. If I were lucky, Grandfather would take me with him. It was a three-day canoe trip, but I enjoyed canoeing with Grandfather. He told the best stories. The black stones from the land with no trees made the sharpest knives. They were not found locally and were highly treasured by the villagers at the east end of the lake.

"Yes," Mother replied, "but he is taking Hassun. Hassun also wants to trade for corn."

Sometimes I think Mother can read my mind. Hassun is the son of my Mother's sister and has seen twenty-one winters. He is good at everything: sports, hunting, story-telling. Sometimes I'm jealous, but mostly I want to grow up just like him.

"I'll fill our pouches with dried meat," Kanti said, her bowl already empty.

Kanti eats faster than I do. She also likes to take charge even though I have seen two more winters than she has. Mother made the pouches for us during the previous winter. They had straps to place over our necks. I had no doubt Kanti would overfill my pouch with more food than I could eat. Kanti had a voracious appetite. Moments later Kanti was hovering over me with spear in one hand and two pouches overflowing with venison jerky in the other hand.

"You ready to go?" she asked.

I grabbed my bag and placed the strap over my head and left arm. We would not be back until late afternoon and the jerky would appease our midday hunger.

"You taking your bow?"

"No, you have your spear. I'm sure that will be sufficient to protect us from any vicious rabbits."

Kanti doesn't go anywhere without her spear. I liked my bow, but unless I was hunting, it was one more item to carry. I had a small rock attached to a stick that I used to kill animals caught in my snares. Grandfather says we should quickly kill such animals to prevent additional pain.

We walked down to the river where many canoes, including our canoe, were pulled up on the shore. Some canoes were large and held many men. They were used to venture into Gitche Gumee. Our canoe was small. We occasionally used it on Gitche Gumee, but it worked better on rivers. The canoe had a red "V" painted on the bow. Below the "V" was a small circle, which gave the impression of an eagle in flight. The Eagle was our family totem.

I enjoyed canoe trips, but today we would be walking. We headed south on the trail that connected the two lakes with no distant shore. At a bend in the trail we turned right and headed into the woods. I enjoyed walking through the woods. The forest was my home. When I walked quietly, I could hear the woods. It spoke to me, like a well-placed whisper. At other times the woods overflowed with music and joy that seemed to come from nowhere and everywhere all at the same time. At the sound of any noise, the music would cease in protest.

"Chogan, do you think rabbits get scared going down a rabbit hole?"

"They get scared when they are not in a rabbit hole," I replied. I had a feeling this would not be a quiet walk in the woods.

"Do rabbits dream?"

"No," I replied.

"You don't know that."

"Then why did you ask me?" I said. "Kanti, you had a bad dream, nothing more, nothing less. It is very unlikely that you will ever have a similar dream."

That seemed to appease Kanti and we continued in silence. Our first snare had a rabbit swinging from a bent sapling. I whacked in the head with my stone club and it ceased struggling.

"That is one rabbit that will never fear another rabbit hole," I said.

"Chogan, I don't think you are taking my dream seriously."

"Sorry."

Nightmares can be scary; but after several hours, logic should overcome fear. No one can fall into a rabbit hole. I was finding it difficult to take Kanti's dream seriously.

"Race you to the next snare," I said.

Kanti took off running as I hoped. She was highly competitive and the race would take her mind off her dream. She was a better athlete than I, and if it were not for my longer legs I wouldn't have been able to keep up. When she came to the log bridge over the river, she almost ran across. I had to hold onto branches on both sides of the river and walk gingerly over the middle. With my longer legs I could have overtaken her in the final stretch, but I let her win.

The snare was tripped but no animal. Animals often escape. After checking all thirty-two snares, we had two rabbits and a duck to show for our efforts. We headed toward our favorite sitting log on the north side of Wagosh Lake. Deer kept the grass well-trimmed and it provided a good view of the lake. That is where we normally ate our lunch. I was glad it was early summer. If it were fall, Kanti would insist on gathering wapatoo tubers from the lake.

I sat down on a fallen log and opened my pouch. As I suspected, Kanti had it filled with more than I could eat. I had no doubt she would eat all of hers.

"Let's eat at the top of the spruce tree." Kanti ran for the tree without giving me an opportunity to object.

The spruce tree was one of the tallest trees in the forest. From the top we could see Gitche Gumee and all of Wagosh Lake. Most animals don't look up, and from the tree top we often see deer, moose and an occasional wolf. It provided a beautiful view. We ate our lunch from the top of the spruce tree almost as often as we ate on our sitting log. I ran after Kanti.

It didn't take us long to reach the top. The spruce offered many handholds and stepping branches. We were familiar with each and every one of them. We sat on our favorite limbs and ate in silence. With such a view, idle chatter adds nothing to the beauty. As usual Kanti finished eating before I did.

"Chogan, have you ever had a dream like that? I mean it was so real."

"Kanti, look how big you are. You have seen many rabbit holes. There is no way you could fall into one of those. I've had nightmares, but that is all they were. I can't even remember any of them. In a few days you will forget all about this."

"I suppose you are right, but this was unlike any nightmare I've had in the past."

"Now we need to head back or Mother will worry," I said.

Chapter Two

"There he is." Grandfather pulled back a large branch that had been obstructing our view. A large bull moose stood knee deep in water eating water lilies near the edge of the pond. Sunlight reflected off its wet hide. If the moose were aware of our presence, it offered no indication. An arrow protruding from the animal's upper left leg suggested we were not the first hunters the moose had encountered.

"Grandfather, the moose is so large. Can my small arrow kill such a massive animal?"

The moose standing before me could easily feed our village for more days than I could count on my fingers, and Mother would still be busy drying meat beside her fire. It would be a great honor if I could bring such a large moose back to our village.

"Chogan, you must place your arrow in the chest, just below the neck. Then it will pierce the heart," Grandfather replied.

I notched my straightest arrow and pulled back on the bowstring. I was using the bow Grandfather had given me. Its arrows had slain many deer. It was the same bow Grandfather used to kill shaggy deer in the land with no trees. The hand grip on the bow was covered with hide from one of the shaggy deer.

"If you hold still the arrow will fly true," Grandfather said. *"You must not let your arm tremble as you release the arrow."* But Grandfather placed his hand on my right shoulder and began shaking my arm. The moose looked up at me with mournful, pleading eyes.

"Why are you shaking my shoulder, Grandfather? My arrow cannot shoot straight."

I opened my eyes; Kanti was shaking my shoulder. It was better than the blunt end of her spear, but I was having such a wonderful dream. I had no doubt the moose would be gone when sleep returned.

"I had another dream," Kanti whispered.

A few glowing embers in the wigwam's fire pit illuminated a tear cascading down Kanti's face. I saw none of the fear in Kanti's eyes as I had after the previous dream. Now I only saw sorrow.

"What was in this dream?" I also whispered. I didn't want to awaken Mother or Grandfather, but my moose skin blanket was warm, and I had no desire to taste the chill that lingered in the air outside our wigwam. Whispering would have to suffice.

"I was stuck in the same rabbit hole. The hole was even darker and more ominous than last night. Chogan, I couldn't see my fingers, but this time I was able to wiggle free. I crawled forward. I don't know why. The moaning became louder, and I could hear a voice pleading to me. Then I got stuck again."

"Then what happened?" I asked.

"I woke up."

"Is that all?" I could tell from the tone of her voice Kanti was holding back. There was more bothering her.

"Chogan, I recognized the voice—it was Takoda!"

It took a moment or two for what Kanti was saying to fully register. Takoda was a boy my age from the land with no trees. His name meant friend-to-everyone in the Sioux language, but he came to the south shore of Gitche Gumee with less than honorable motives. Eventually we became close friends. I wished him no harm.

"Kanti, it is nice to hear from Takoda. Can I go back to sleep now? I was having a wonderful dream about a large moose." My mind was still fogged with sleep.

"Takoda needs our help." Kanti shook my shoulder again to ensure I was listening.

"Just because you dream about Takoda does not mean he's in trouble." I was becoming irritated.

"You don't know that."

"Look, Kanti, I lack the wisdom of the owl, and I don't think well in the dark. Can't this wait until morning?"

"Okay, but I'm going to help Takoda with or without your assistance."

Kanti returned to her sleeping bench. At least she was no longer tearful. Now she was angry—at me. But there was nothing I could do even if Takoda were in need of help. He lived in the land with no trees. The full moon could come and go several times before we could travel to such a faraway place. I did find it strange that Kanti had the same dream twice. That was a thought best pondered in the morning.

Sleep came easily for Kanti. Discussing her dream must have been therapeutic. I, on the other hand, fidgeted most of the night. I couldn't banish Kanti's dreams from my mind. When I awoke in the morning all the sleeping benches were empty and the sleeping blankets neatly folded. My sleeping bench never looked that tidy.

"Good morning, Chogan," Mother said. "I trust the chirping birds did not disturb your sleep." Mother gave me a bowl of steamed rice. It was cold, but would have been warm if I had arisen with the others.

"Where is everyone?" I could see no activity around the neighboring wigwams. The fire pits where women normally dried meat and prepared meals were deserted.

"The Winnebago traders arrived late last night. Everyone is at the beach inspecting their merchandise."

The traders belonged to the Winnebago Indian tribe that dwelled along the other lake with no distant shore. They were one of the few local tribes that spoke the Sioux language. Since the Winnebago also spoke our tongue, they were natural traders. Their arrival always filled our village with excitement.

"Mother, have people from the distant villages begun to arrive?"

"Some of them arrived early this morning. I assume more will arrive by evening."

The Winnebago traders traveled to faraway lands in big canoes where they gathered rare and exotic merchandise such as obsidian, pipestone, woven rugs, beads, and other desirable items. We would soon have many visitors from inland villages. If I wished to avoid the crowds and view their merchandise up close I would have to eat fast.

"Is Kanti trading her fish net?" I asked.

"I assume so," Mother replied. "She took it with her when she left."

Kanti spent most of the winter making a large fish net from basswood twine. It was a beautiful net and would reap a bounty of goods if she were a shrewd trader. Perhaps the excitement of the Winnebago traders will have taken her mind off her dreams. I quickly finished my wild rice.

"Mother, I'll be at the beach." I didn't linger to hear Mother's reply. Unlike Kanti, I had nothing to trade, but I didn't want to miss any excitement. I found many people gathering around four large canoes. The canoes were three times the length of Grandfather's canoe, and I would have difficulty touching both sides at its widest section. I assumed the four men standing in front of the canoes were needed to paddle such a large canoe.

A wide variety of strange and exotic merchandise filled their canoes. The treasure of items obviously came from many lands. I didn't recognize some of the people who gathered around the canoes. Word must have spread to the neighboring villages. There would be many more people by evening.

The Winnebago merchants' clothing differed from our clothing, making them easy to recognize in the crowd. I walked over to the first canoe where two merchants were discussing the merits of obsidian and pipestone with my cousin Hassun. Neither side appeared eager to close the deal. Hassun had several coils of basswood rope he was willing to trade. I have been told that basswood rope was a rare commodity in the land with no trees. If Hassun were to obtain a good bargain, he could trade the obsidian and pipestone for corn when he and Grandfather visited the village at the far end of Gitche Gumee.

I pushed my way through the crowd to the second canoe where Kanti was talking to a Winnebago boy not much older than I. The boy was wearing a breastplate made of dyed porcupine quills and beads crafted from colorful seeds. A variety of feathers adorned his hair. I assumed all were for sale. A man who appeared to be the boy's father was chatting with several villagers who were attracted by knives made from sharpened obsidian.

"Chogan, this is Nawkaw. He thinks he may have met Takoda."

I am shy and slow at making friends but not Kanti. She was behaving as if Nawkaw were an old friend. Kanti had her fish net draped over her shoulder. Perhaps making friends with Nawkaw would sweeten any barter, although I suspected Nawkaw's father would oversee all trades.

"It was during the spring of last year when we traded in the land with no trees," Nawkaw said with a smile. "My father and I met a great chief among the Sioux Nations. He had a grandson who appeared similar to Kanti's description of your friend."

Nawkaw had an engaging personality no doubt honed from his business experience. Perhaps I was being too cynical, but I questioned his sincerity.

"It could have been our friend," I replied, "but the Sioux are a large nation and they have many chiefs."

Nawkaw nodded in agreement. "That is true," he said. "Tomorrow we depart for the land with no trees. If I see the boy again I can give him a message."

"That's very thoughtful," I replied. "We will provide a message before you leave."

"Kanti, we need to talk." I pulled Kanti aside. She was reluctant to leave her new-found friend, but after some physical encouragement I maneuvered her beyond the hearing of the young Winnebago.

"You didn't tell Nawkaw about your dreams, did you?" Kanti was impulsive and often spoke without thinking. Telling people about falling into a rabbit hole would only bring ridicule.

"Not yet," Kanti replied. "What's your problem? Dreams don't have to be a secret."

It was obvious Kanti was still angry with me. She could be stubborn at times. If she believed Takoda was hiding at the bottom of a rabbit hole, no amount of logic or reasoning would persuade her otherwise. I still felt compelled to try.

"Kanti, last night I told you I would give your dreams some thought when it became daylight and I have. Rabbit holes are for rabbits, not people. There is no way you would fit in a rabbit hole."

"That's why I got stuck," Kanti replied.

This would not be easy. I wondered if discussing Kanti's dreams was worth the effort. It appeared unlikely I would change her mind, and there was little Kanti could do even if she remained convinced of her dream's authenticity.

"Suppose Takoda was at the bottom of a rabbit hole," I said. "How do you suggest we help him, send a rabbit after him?" That had her stumped for a moment, and my sarcasm sailed over her head. Perhaps she would surrender to reason.

"Remember the Medicine Woman from Kitchiminiss?" Kanti asked. "I saw her this morning. She's here in our village."

"She provided medicine when Takoda's wound became infected," I replied. "That won't help Takoda now. That's assuming Takoda even needs our help. The Medicine Woman is good with salves and potions, not dreams. It'll take more than a salve to extract Takoda from a rabbit hole."

The previous summer Kanti and I found Takoda with an arrow embedded in his left thigh. The wound was infected and Takoda would have died without the salve the Medicine Woman provided. But Takoda returned to his home in the land with no trees. Neither the Medicine Woman nor Kanti and I could provide further help.

"I don't care. I'm still going to talk to the Medicine Woman."

"She'll expect a gift," I replied.

"We snared two rabbits yesterday. We can spare one of them."

"How will you explain that to Mother and Grandfather?" I asked.

"We have many visitors in our village. We'll tell Mother we gave the rabbit to a hungry family. Grandfather always says we must help the needy."

I was not thrilled with the *we* part of Kanti's plan, but I was sure Grandfather would support our gift to the needy, not that the Medicine Woman was that much in need. The Medicine Woman was a wise woman. I had to admit I was interested in any wisdom she had to offer.

Kanti took off running toward our wigwam. She seldom walked anywhere. After a few moments she returned with rabbit in hand. "You ready?" she asked.

"What did Mother say about the rabbit?"

"She wasn't there," Kanti replied. "I think she's at the beach with everyone one else. You can explain the rabbit later. Let's find the Medicine Woman."

I don't know why explaining the missing rabbit was now my problem. Talking to the Medicine Woman better not be a waste of time. I was not optimistic.

"Where do we find the Medicine Woman?" I asked.

"She made a temporary lean-to down by the river."

The river formed the eastern boundary to our village and spilled its water into Gitche Gumee. The river's mouth provided a safe haven for canoes arriving from the big lake. Any personal belongings left in canoes were usually secure, but it was still not unusual for visitors to set up temporary shelters within view of their canoes.

The Medicine Woman's lean-to was not hard to find. The simple structure consisted of two upright poles with Y's at the top. A longer pole stretched horizontally between the two Y's. A deerskin covering protected the inhabitant from only the mildest weather. The many medicinal herbs and charms hanging from the poles confirm the occupant's identity.

The Medicine Woman was a large woman and her frame filled a greater portion of the lean-to. She was sitting on a log she had dragged into her lean-to for that purpose and was stirring a potion in a birch bark container. I waited until she looked up.

"May we speak to you?" I asked.

"You already have," She replied. "Sit down, my children, and you can speak some more. Children seldom find an old woman worthy of conversation. I am honored."

We sat cross-legged on the ground in front of her. She seemed pleased with our visit, and I felt it would be disrespectful to bluntly state our purpose. That would come after small talk.

"You have a very pretty necklace," I said. I had no doubt the necklace was a recent trade with the Winnebago. It had multicolored porcupine quills separated by large red seeds.

"I made many good trades with the merchants. When I return to Kitchi-miniss I can trade my goods for more practical items such as corn and wild rice. Even an old woman needs to eat."

"You will also need to eat while you are a guest in our village," I said. "We brought you a rabbit." I passed the rabbit to the Medicine Woman. She graciously accepted our small gift. It was not as substantial as the large beaver we had given her the year before.

"You two look familiar. How do I know you?" the woman asked. "I seldom forget a face."

"We visited you last summer at Kitchi-miniss," I replied. "My name is Chogan and this is my sister, Kanti."

"Yes, I remember now. You brought me a nice fat beaver, and I gave you a salve for your friend who had an arrow in his thigh. How is your friend? Is he doing well?"

"I was able to remove the arrow and your salve resolved his infection," I replied. "He was lucky we found him in the woods otherwise he would have surely died."

"Takoda's wound healed nicely, but we think he is in trouble again," Kanti explained.

I wished Kanti wouldn't use the word *we* so frequently. *We* did not think Takoda was in danger. I had little doubt that Takoda was enjoying life in the shade of those purple hills that reached up to kiss the sky. Someday I will rest in the shade of those purple hills.

The Medicine Woman listened intently as Kanti explained her dreams. Kanti was a good story teller. The current account of her dreams was far more dramatic and embellished than the tale she had offered to me. But no matter how she told the story it still left her stuck inside a rabbit hole that was ten sizes too small.

When Kanti finished describing her dreams, the old woman leaned back, closed her eyes, and began to rock. If not for her slow rocking motion, I would have assumed she was asleep. As I expected, we were wasting a good rabbit. I should never have given Kanti permission to talk with the Medicine Woman, not that Kanti thought she needed my permission. I was about to stand up and leave when the Medicine Woman opened her eyes.

"It is well that you have come to me. You saved Takoda's life and now his spirit has bonded with you. You feel its energy. Takoda's spirit has reached out to you over a long distance. It would not have done so unless Takoda was in grave danger. You saved Takoda in the past and the spirit hopes you will again rise to the occasion."

"Are we too late?" Kanti asked. "Has he already left for the spirit world?"

"The fact that you continue to have dream tells me he is still alive and reaching out to you," the woman replied. "For how long, I do not know."

That was not what I wanted to hear. Kanti did not need further encouragement. If Takoda truly were in danger, we could not save him. The Medicine Woman was promoting needless worry.

"If this is all true, why isn't Takoda's spirit reaching out to me? I was just as responsible for saving Takoda's life as Kanti. Perhaps more so." I felt I needed to add some reality to the discussion. I couldn't let the Medicine Woman's thoughts go unchallenged.

"Tell me your dreams," the woman said. "They are not similar?"

"I don't have dreams."

"You do too," Kanti replied. "You told me you had a dream about a moose."

I had forgotten that dream. Unlike Kanti's dream mine was pleasant and enjoyable, without voices or hidden meaning. I would have shot the moose if Kanti hadn't awakened me. That would have made my dream even more enjoyable. Grandfather said my arrow would have pierced the moose's heart if I hit the moose in the chest just below the neck.

"Tell me about your dream," the woman said. It was not a request. It felt like a command. There was no way I could politely ignore the request.

"It was an ordinary dream," I said. "Grandfather and I were hunting and came upon a huge bull moose. The moose had an arrow in its rear leg. Some other hunter had tried to bring down the moose before me and had failed. Grandfather said if my arrow hit the moose in the chest just below the neck it would pierce the moose's heart."

"Did you kill the moose?" the medicine woman asked.

"No. Grandfather said my arrow would fly true if I held my arm steady, but then he placed his hand on my shoulder and shook it so I could not hold my arm still."

"Then what happened?" the woman asked.

"Kanti woke me up."

"So, you had a dream about a moose the same time your sister was having a dream about a rabbit hole and a plea for help."

"Yes, but my dream was pleasant. It had nothing to do with Takoda." I didn't like the direction the conversation was going.

"You said the moose had an arrow protruding from its upper rear leg."

I nodded in agreement.

"On which side of the moose was the arrow?"

"On the left side," I replied. I couldn't see what difference that made.

"You told me your friend, Takoda, once had an arrow lodged in his thigh. Which thigh was it?"

I felt like someone had kicked me in the stomach. It had to be coincidental. Takoda had two legs. The arrow had to be one of them. Then I remembered the mournful look on the moose's face when we made eye contact.

"Takoda had an arrow embedded in his left thigh!" Kanti stared at me with her I told you so look. I was still not convinced.

"Chogan, Takoda's spirit has reached out to you, but found resistance. Your Grandfather's spirit recognized the presence of Takoda's spirit. He shook your shoulder to prevent you from harming your friend."

"Why do my dreams always end with me getting stuck in the hole?" Kanti asked. "There is never an end to my dreams."

"Your dreams only portray what the spirit world knows of your future. What lies beyond the rabbit hole is uncharted territory. You must shape your destiny for better or for worse. Your friend is in grave trouble and only you can save him."

After some more small talk we thanked the Medicine Woman for her time and departed. I still didn't agree with her assessment, but neither could I prove her wrong. When it came to her herbs and potions everyone had the utmost confidence in her abilities, but interpreting dreams was beyond her normal expertise. I was not sure I believe in these spirits.

"So, what are we going to do to help Takoda? Kanti asked. She had her hands on her hips in her typical defiant stance. It was unlikely she would agree with any of my suggestions.

"There isn't much we can do," I replied. "Perhaps Takoda's spirit will provide guidance in a future dream." I was assuming there would be no further dreams, and we would be done with this matter.

"Chogan, you aren't taking this seriously. I'm going to discuss this with my Winnebago friend. At least he is willing to help. I'll have him make inquiries about Takoda when he reaches the land without trees."

Kanti was still angry with me, but the Winnebago merchants were visiting our village, and I had not seen all they had to offer. Tonight the men would sit around the fire and tell stories. Boys my age wouldn't be invited, but I would be listening from a distance. I didn't want to have Kanti's dreams interfere with an exciting day. I parted company with Kanti.

I spent the rest of the afternoon inspecting the merchandize offered by the Winnebago traders and catching up with friends from the neighboring villages. We had enough boys my age for a spirited baggataway match. Our team consisted of boys from our village. We competed against the visitors. I would like to say we won, but we were severely outnumbered. All I had to show for my efforts was a bloody nose after one of my own teammates elbowed me in the face.

The population of our village had doubled in size by evening, and everyone was in a festive mood. The carcasses of several deer roasting over communal fires suggested that no one would go hungry. Mother and a neighbor woman were in charge of one of the fires. I had Mother cut a large piece of venison for me. She stabbed it with a short stick and passed it to me.

"Where is Kanti?" she asked. Kanti usually tagged along after me, so this was not a surprising question.

"Last time I saw her, she was hanging out with the son of a Winnebago merchant."

"You need to find her," Mother said. "Make sure she gets something to eat."

"Yes, Mother."

"It is also starting to get dark. I want the two of you to stay together."

"Yes, Mother."

I never have to worry about Kanti getting enough to eat. Food was plentiful and she was an eating machine. I didn't know how she stayed so skinny. It didn't take long to find her. She was chatting with the Winnebago boy. His name was Nawkaw if my memory served me correctly.

"Mother wants to know if you found something to eat."

"Nawkaw and I ate some venison. Nawkaw says venison tastes similar to tatanka," Kanti replied.

"What's tatanka?" I asked. I didn't want to sound stupid, but I had never heard of tatanka, and I knew most of the animals that inhabited our forest.

"Tatanka is what the Sioux call the shaggy deer that Grandfather always talks about," Kanti replied. "Nawkaw says only the front half of the tatanka is shaggy, but they are thick in the chest like a moose, and their legs are short—just like Grandfather described them."

I couldn't visualize a short-legged moose with a shaggy front half. If Grandfather had not provided a similar description, I would have accused Nawkaw of fabricating his story. Someday I will travel to the land with no trees and see these beasts firsthand.

"Mother says we must stay together now that it is dark," I said. "The elders are gathering around the fire to share the friendship pipe. I plan to listen to their stories."

"Can Nawkaw come with us?" Kanti asked.

"There is nothing to stop him," I replied. I regretted my words as soon as I said them. I was being rude. For all I knew, Nawkaw was a nice person. I was letting my displeasure with Kanti and her dreams diminish my hospitality toward a visitor in our village.

"We would be happy to have you come with us," I said. "Whenever we have many guests in our village, the village elders gather around a fire and smoke a friendship pipe. I was once a guest at a friendship circle and was allowed to smoke the pipe. It was a horrible experience."

I led Nawkaw and Kanti toward our usual spot in the bushes. We were close enough to the fire circle to hear what was being said but outside of the light from the fire pit. As long as we whispered, no one knew we were there.

"The first part is boring," I told Nawkaw. "Everyone introduces himself and says great things about his village. Then he takes a puff on the pipe."

"After that everyone tells stories," Kanti said. "That is the best part of the evening."

"My father is a good story teller," Nawkaw said. "I believe he is sitting next to your grandfather."

We waited patiently while the pipe was passed around. I had heard the introductions before and I knew all about their villages. I wanted to hear their tales. The pipe slowly made its way around the circle. There was no way to rush someone who was extoling the virtues of his village.

"Now they will tell their tales," Kanti whispered as the pipe completed its circuit and Hassun stood to speak. "He's our cousin."

Hassun told of spearing a large sturgeon that pulled his canoe around the lake for most of the day. Another man stood up and told of tracking a large moose in deep snow for three days. He was able to kill the moose and provide meat for his starving village. One by one the men in the circle rose to tell tales of their life accomplishments. Finally it was Grandfather's turn.

"Grandfather will tell of his visit to the land with no trees when he was little older than I am," I told Nawkaw. I had heard Grandfather tell his story many times, and it never failed to leave me in awe.

Grandfather slowly rose and waited until all were quiet. Then he told of traveling west for several full moons to the land with no trees, where he met a young man named Wambleeska.

"Wambleeska means White Eagle in your language," Nawkaw told us.

"I know," I replied. "He is a great chief of the Sioux Nation." I don't know why I had to add that. Perhaps I

was a bit jealous of Nawkaw. He had been to the land
with no trees; I have only heard Grandfather's tales.

Grandfather told how Wambleeska and he explored
the land swathed with grass. He told of the shaggy deer
that were thick in the chest like a moose and covered the
land for as far as one could see. He told of purple hills
that rose up to kiss the sky. Grandfather sat down at the
end of his tale. Grandfather was last to speak and the men
began to disperse.

"Is it really true that there are no trees?" Kanti asked.
It was hard to imagine a land without any trees.

"There are a few trees along the rivers and in the
purple hills," Nawkaw replied. "Most of the land is
covered with grass, but even the grass is not as thick or
green as what you have here."

"It is a strange land," I said.

"There is an even stranger land in the purple hills
where mud boils and water spurts up higher than your
tallest tree," Nawkaw added. "The Sioux consider it
sacred ground."

I assumed Nawkaw was telling a tall tale of his own.
Mud does not boil and water flows down, not up. We
parted ways and Kanti and I headed for our wigwam. It
was getting late. Tomorrow our village routine would
return to normal. The Winnebago merchants would be
gone and Grandfather would be canoeing to the east end
of Gitche Gumee with Hassun. Grandfather would be
gone for three days. I would miss his presence in the
wigwam, but Kanti and I would be busy tending our
snares.

"Where's your fish net?" I hadn't noticed before, but
it was no longer draped over Kanti's shoulder. "Did you
trade it for something good?" The merchants were

leaving early in the morning. If Kanti wished to make a trade, she would have done it by now.

"You will find out soon enough," she replied. She was obviously still angry with me. Sometimes Kanti could hold a grudge for extended periods. I was hoping this was not one of those times.

Kanti entered our wigwam, but I waited for Grandfather's return. I had some questions I wished to ask. I did not have to wait long. He and Hassun were conversing, no doubt discussing the trip in the morning. I waited patiently until Hassun departed for his wigwam.

"Grandfather," I said when he looked up. "When you traveled to the land with no trees, did you ever see mud boil or water spout up higher than the tallest tree?" I feared he might laugh at my question, but he merely rubbed his chin.

"I never saw what you mentioned, but my friend spoke of such a place hidden away in the purple hills. Wambleeska was not one to tell false tales. The Sioux consider the area holy ground. We were to visit the boiling mud, but I had to return to our homeland before winter made travel dangerous. Tomorrow's trip to the east shore of Gitche Gumee should be much easier. It will still take all of three days. I trust you will take good care of your sister and mother while I am gone. We will be using Hassun's canoe because its larger size better weathers Gitche Gumee's waves. You will have our canoe available if needed."

"Yes, Grandfather." I entered our wigwam and crawled onto my sleeping bench. Tomorrow would be a busy day.

Chapter Three

"Chogan, wake up. You need to check your snares."

I forced open my eyes, hoping to see darkness that would suggest it was still night and Mother's voice had been part of a cruel dream. I saw light streaming down from the smoke hole at the top of our wigwam—it was morning. But why was Mother awakening me. Kanti normally took perverse satisfaction in that chore. I looked around; all the sleeping benches were empty. That was no surprise. Grandfather and Hassun were canoeing toward the east end of Gitche Gumee and mother was always up before me. I staggered out of the wigwam.

"Where's Kanti?" I asked.

"She must be talking to one of her friends," Mother replied. "She was up before me."

Mother gave me some porridge that I ate with my two fingers. Normally Kanti would have everything prepared for checking our snares. She would have our pouches packed with a lunch and would be hovering impatiently while I ate breakfast. I had mixed feelings about her absence.

"I think Kanti is still angry with me for not taking her dreams seriously," I said. "Perhaps it would be best if I checked my snares without her." I had done that in the past before Kanti talked Mother into letting her go with me.

"Chogan, I don't know what these dreams are all about, but I want you to find your sister and apologize to her or do whatever it takes to settle your disagreement. I will not tolerate any disagreements that remain to greet the rising sun."

"Yes, Mother."

I finished my breakfast and set out to find my sister. She was most likely with her best friend, Namid. I headed toward Namid's wigwam. Namid was sitting on a log helping her mother weave mats out of cattail reeds. I offered a polite hello to Namid's mother and then turned toward Namid.

"Namid, do you know where I can find Kanti?"

"Kanti's not here," Namid replied.

I got the impression Namid was not providing the whole truth. I had asked if she knew where I could find Kanti. She merely replied that Kanti was not here. That I could see for myself. I had little doubt Namid knew where I could find her. If Namid's mother were not present, I was sure I could make Namid talk, although Grandfather would not approve of my methods.

I wandered about the village, but found no sign of Kanti. She could be inside any of the wigwams and I wouldn't find her. I walked down to the beach thinking she may have been talking to Nawkaw, but several people said the Winnebago merchants left at first light.

"Mother, I looked everywhere and I can't find her."

"Have you talked to Namid?" Mother asked. She looked worried.

"If Namid knows anything, she isn't telling," I replied.

I looked under Kanti's sleeping bench for anything that might suggest her whereabouts. Her fish net was gone, but I couldn't find any trinkets or jewelry that she might have received in trade. She had hinted the previous evening that I would know today what she received in trade. I found nothing.

"Mother, Kanti's spear is gone. Maybe she decided to check our snares without me."

Kanti knew her way around the woods as well as I did and was capable of checking the snares without me, but that was carrying her grudge too far. Further checking revealed her lunch pouch was missing.

"Chogan, try to catch up with her. I expect to see both of you return together—and cheerfully."

"Yes, Mother."

I didn't bother adding jerky to my deerskin pouch. I would have to skip lunch. Kanti had a significant head start. I grabbed the stone hammer I used to dispatch rabbits or other game caught in my traps and headed down the trail. I ran the first segment of the trail, but once I turned into the woods, brush and other obstacles made running impossible. I assumed Kanti would have to stop and reset snares and deal with trapped animals. Sooner or later I would catch up with her. I crossed the log bridge over the river and headed toward the first snare.

I had set the hanging noose snare next to a small pond frequented by ducks. It was a simple snare that looped around the duck's neck and strangled the duck as it resisted. I was pleased to see that it had snared a fat mallard duck. It had to be a recent catch or Kanti would have tied it to her waist and reset the snare. I removed the duck from the snare; the body was stiff. It had been dead for some time. If Kanti wasn't checking our snares, then where was she? There had to be a logical explanation, but none came to mind. I had to admit I was becoming worried.

I ran toward our village and didn't slow to a walk until the village was in sight. I needed to catch my breath before I talked to Mother. I was hoping I would find Kanti casually talking to Mother. Unfortunately, that was not the case. Mother was staring off into the distance, lost in thought. She didn't notice as I approached.

"She isn't checking our snares," I said. "None of the traps was reset. We did catch a find duck." I held up the mallard duck hoping to distract mother, but she was not interested.

"Look around the village again, Chogan. We need to find her. Talk with Namid. She will know where Kanti is."

"Namid was rather evasive when I asked her earlier, but I'll talk to her again."

"I'm coming with you," Mother said. "When I find Kanti, she better have a good excuse for her absence." I wasn't sure if Mother was speaking out of anger or fear. Kanti was always the dependable child. My behavior was more likely to give Mother grief.

Namid's wigwam was near the river. She was still sitting on her log weaving mats with her mother when we arrived. Namid began to fidget when she noticed I had returned with reinforcements. I stepped back so Mother could do the talking. When angered or worried, she was far more intimidating than I am.

"Kanti is missing," Mother said. "We were hoping Namid might know where we can find her." The question was directed to Namid's mother, but all eyes were now on Namid. Namid began to squirm. It was as good as a confession.

"It's possible that she left with the Winnebago merchants," Namid replied.

"They kidnapped her?" Mother asked. Mother is usually a pillar of strength in a crisis, but her voice began to quiver. I was sure she feared the worst.

"I didn't see her leave but if she did go with the Winnebago merchants, she did so willingly," Namid replied.

"Why would she do that?" Mother asked.

"The Winnebago merchants are traveling to the land with no trees," Namid said. "Kanti told me she needed to help a friend of hers. I didn't understand all of it."

"Kanti had some wild dreams that made her think Takoda was in danger," I said. Namid looked relieved when all eyes focused on me. Mother made me recite the events of the last several days. Part of the time Mother had her eyes closed. She appeared deep in sleep, but I knew she was deep in thought. Mother was never one to panic. She was weighing all the options and devising a plan of action.

"Chogan, Grandfather will be gone for three days," Mother said. "You will have to go after Kanti and bring her back. We have extra pemmican you can take with you to eat. Stop at any of the villages along the way, and they will provide more food. That is our custom. If you are not back in three days, I will send Grandfather and Hassun after you."

I was filled with guilt. Maybe if I had been more understanding Kanti might not have joined the Winnebago merchants. But finding her would not be easy.

"Mother, they have a half-day head start, and there are four strong men in each canoe. It's unlikely I'll catch them in three days, but I won't return home without Kanti even if I have to track them all the way to the land with no trees. I'll leave a trail for Grandfather and Hassun to follow."

"I'll get the pemmican, but you must leave quickly."

Chapter Four

It was late in the day when I pushed my canoe into the river and paddled toward the river's mouth. Mother filled my shoulder pouch with dried meat, and I had enough pemmican to last several days. If I ran short of food, villages along the way would provide assistance. It was our tradition to help those in need. My young age should intensify their generosity.

The canoe felt empty without Kanti in the front. I knelt in the center of the canoe. If I paddled from the rear, the canoe would tip upward without Kanti's weight to counterbalance mine. I missed her already.

I packed Kanti's kneeling pad and paddle in the front of the canoe. We would need them on the return trip. Perhaps I was being overly optimistic, but I was consumed with guilt and the optimism made me feel better. Kanti joined the merchants because I didn't take her dreams seriously. They may have seemed frivolous to me, but to Kanti the dreams were real. I paddled on.

I turned northwest when the river opened into Gitche Gumee. The lake was calm, which is often the case in the evening when the wind subsides. My canoe was small and designed for navigating rivers. If the water were to become rough, I would have to wait out the storm on shore. The Winnebago merchants paddled larger canoes that could weather Gitche Gumee's bigger waves. Four strong men propelled each canoe. It was unlikely I would overtake them before they reached the western end of Gitche Gumee. Once they entered the woods, they would be almost impossible to track. If I were lucky the Winnebago merchants might stop at one or two villages along the way, assuming they didn't visit those villages on their way east. If they did stop, they wouldn't linger long, since they had sold most of their merchandise.

By early evening I passed a cluster of tall hills and then headed west into the sun. A few clouds would have been nice, but the sky was clear. I could only look into the sun for brief moments. If a merchant's canoe were in front of me I wouldn't have noticed, not that I expected to see them. They were a day ahead of me and increasing their distance. At some point I would have to admit defeat and turn back.

I ceased paddling briefly to rest my arms. Other than the sound of an occasional wave lapping at my canoe, I sat in silence. I cut a piece of pemmican with my bone knife and elevated it to my mouth. I was famished and my mouth began to water in anticipation before I began to chew. Pemmican is a mixture of ground dried meat and rendered fat. It is often used on long trips because it remains edible even after several full moons have passed. I expected to count my journey in days not full moons.

When I resumed paddling, the sun was lower in the sky. I watched as the yellow sun turned orange and then red. The few clouds remaining in the sky glowed with yellows and reds. On an ordinary day this would have been a beautiful sunset, but this was not an ordinary day. I wondered if Kanti were enjoying the same sunset. I paddled on.

A few brighter stars made their appearance. Maybe the merchants would beach their canoes for the night. They were not in a hurry. I was. I paddled into the darkness. Moonlight would have been nice, but the starlight was sufficient to see the shore and that was all I needed. If fog developed, my day would be over. Fortunately, the air remained clear. I could follow the shoreline. That provided the greatest safety, but the shoreline contained many bays and small peninsulas. Grandfather says the shortest distance between two points is a straight line, and I was in a hurry. As long as I kept Giwaydin Ahnung, the star that always points north, over my right shoulder I would be paddling west.

Grandfather taught me how to find Giwaydin Ahnung using two pointer stars. He spoke of a great bear in the sky. Three stars named Moosebird, Chickadee, and Robin hunted the bear throughout the summer. I used to feel sorry for the bear until a bear almost killed Kanti and me. It is no fun being hunted.

***

To find out more about Moosebird, Chickadee & Robin see Chogan's web page at: http://winnebago-merchant.com/skyhunters.htm

***

To help stay awake I searched for other familiar stars. Grandfather knew many legends for such stars. Grandfather told about Fisher who was a small animal but a great hunter. Hunting was difficult during the early years because it was always winter. "We will go where earth is closest to Skyland," Fisher told his friends. "If we can break through to Skyland, where it is always warm, we will bring warmth down to earth."

Otter, Wolverine, and Lynx followed Fisher up the mountain. When they reached the top, they jumped up against Skyland. Wolverine broke through first, and Fisher followed him through the crack into a warm paradise filled with plants and flowers.

The Sky people rushed from their wigwams saying, "The earth people are stealing our warm weather!" Wolverine escaped, but Fisher lingered to enlarge the crack into Skyland. The Sky-People shot many arrows at Fisher and one of the arrows fatally wounded Fisher, but the great Gitche Manitou took pity on Fisher and healed his wounds.

The great Gitche Manitou placed Fisher in the bowl of the drinking gourd. Each autumn as the bowl of the gourd tips, Fisher falls toward Earth. The Sky-People patch the crack in the sky and winter comes. Then in spring Fisher climbs back into the sky and reopens the crack, giving us summer.

It was getting late. Even with mentally retelling Grandfather's stories, I was finding it difficult to keep my eyes open. I would need sleep if I were to paddle the following day. I dragged my paddle on the left side, and the canoe turned toward the shore. In the starlight I could see large boulders and sandstone cliffs neither of which was hospitable to a weary traveler. I paddled on until I came upon a small cove with a sandy beach. When my paddle struck sand, I stepped out of the canoe and dragged it the rest of the way. I didn't want to hit a submerged rock. Fifty paces from the water's edge the sandy beach changed to dense forest. The trees would provide shelter from any breeze, but without a birch bark torch visibility would be down to nothing. I decided to spend my night on the beach. I had my moose skin blanket to keep me warm. If that was insufficient I could build a fire.

I turned over my canoe and then propped it up with a "Y" shaped stick. There was just enough room for me to crawl under the canoe. It wasn't the best shelter, but it would prevent dew from accumulating on my clothing. I wrapped myself in my moose skin blanket and quickly fell asleep.

The sun was shining in my eyes when I awoke—I slept longer than I had planned. I ate a strip of dried venison and then pushed my canoe into the water. I was again lucky to have calm water. Two days in a row was unusual for Gitche Gumee.

I stopped at a small village as the sun reached high in the sky. It was a long shot, but I was hoping someone in the village would have word of the Winnebago merchants. My reception was hospitable as was our custom but still lukewarm until I mentioned Grandfather. He's a highly respected Ojibway elder and well known along the shores of Gitche Gumee. His name immediately brought offers of dried venison, which I graciously accepted. According to the villagers, the Winnebago merchants briefly stopped at their village on the previous day. A young Ojibway girl matching Kanti's description was with them. One of the villagers produced a fish net he had obtained from a Winnebago merchant; it was the net Kanti had made. It all made sense now. Kanti traded her net for transportation to the land with no trees.

It was probably a one way trip, since Kanti didn't have a second net to barter for the trip home. I am told the land with no trees is a large place. It was unlikely Kanti would find Takoda even if she were to complete her journey. Kanti acts impulsively, she no doubt had not considered those difficulties.

It was depressing to know I was a full day behind the merchants. I thanked my hosts for their dried venison and hospitality and then continued on my way. I had one advantage over the Winnebago merchants that might shorten their lead by a day, but would that be sufficient to overtake the merchants?

If I continued west I would encounter a large peninsula that extended far into Gitche Gumee. It would take an average voyager more than a day to navigate around the peninsula. Fortunately, I was not an average voyager. Grandfather once showed me a river that almost sliced through the peninsula. It would require a short portage, but if I used the river I could save a full day of paddling. The merchants' canoes were too large and heavy for the small river. They would be forced around the peninsula. Many rivers discharge their water into Gitche Gumee. I now had to find the right one.

I headed across a great bay. In the distance I could see the large peninsula jutting into the lake. I headed for a spot that I hoped was south of the river. I wouldn't have time to scout both directions. I needed luck on my side. Judging from the position of the sun, it was midday when I reached the peninsula. I turned north hoping I'd see something familiar. What I saw was familiar. The shoreline was covered with large boulders and tree trunks that had been washed by endless waves. It looked like any other shore on Gitche Gumee. I explored two small rivers, but quickly discovered they went nowhere. The third river looked more familiar. I pulled the canoe up on the shore. Burnt wood along the riverbank suggested other travelers had used the river. I gathered some rocks and placed them one on top of another until I had created a pile easily seen from the lake. Then I carved a large "V" on the trunk of a tree. A round circle at the base of the "V" completed my flying eagle. It would be easy for Grandfather and Hassun to find if they were following me, as I assumed they would.

I ate a snack of pemmican and then headed up the river. The river was filled with large rocks and tree stumps. I could paddle around most of them. My canoe was light and short. It was made for rivers. There was no way the merchants could navigate the river with their large canoes. I still had to drag the canoe through a few spots where the water was shallow. It wasn't until I reached a small lake that I knew for sure I had the correct river passage.

I liked rivers and small lakes. Gitche Gumee was devoid of life other than the omnipresent seagulls, but rivers and lakes were filled with wildlife. Every log had one or more painted turtles absorbing the afternoon sun. Colorful wood ducks played in the shallows. If I were lucky I might catch a glimpse of a deer drinking from the water far ahead of me. Deer are shy and quickly disappear into the woods once they see me. I had to fight the urge to relax and enjoy the journey. I pushed on.

Eventually, the water trail dwindled to nothing. My canoe could no longer offer transportation. I pulled up to shore where a well-marked trail led into the woods. I had to make the rest of the journey on foot. If I remembered correctly it was not a long portage to the other side of the peninsula. I carved our flying eagle mark on a nearby tree for Grandfather and Hassun to find.

I bound Kanti's paddle and mine at the middle to form an "X." Then I lashed the paddles to the canoe. I placed the kneeling pads around my shoulders and then lifted the canoe over my head. I gently lowered the canoe until the paddles rested on my shoulders. Once I got the canoe properly balanced, I headed down the trail. Occasionally, I had to tip the front of the canoe upward, so I could follow the trail. Fortunately it was well marked, but it was still difficult. I hated portages. Canoes were made for paddling, not for carrying. At least the trail was flat and wide. I walked as quickly as I could.

It wasn't long before my shoulders began to ache. If I remembered right, when I had made this portage with Grandfather, he had carried the canoe and I carried the supplies. Now I was carrying the canoe, and the supplies of pemmican and dried meat were strapped to my waist. I made several stops along the way to rest. I was beginning to wonder how much time I was actually saving by cutting across the peninsula. I was never as happy as when I saw Gitche Gumee in the distance. I dragged the canoe across the last forty paces of beach sand until it again gently floated in the water. I checked for leaks, but found none. It was time for another lunch break. My body was using lots of energy, and I had eaten accordingly. Now I was getting low on pemmican. Fortunately, I would soon reach a large Ojibway village nestled among many islands. It was home to my cousin Aranck. I was hoping he would take pity on me when I explained my mission and would provide me with additional food.

I left my mark on a tree for Grandfather and Hassun to find and then pushed my canoe into the water. Paddling a canoe is still strenuous, but it was not as taxing as carrying the canoe on my shoulder. Canoes were made to float on water—not on shoulders.

I saw nothing that looked like Winnebago merchants. It was possible that I was now ahead of them, or they could still be in front of me. I couldn't afford to wait and find out. Storm clouds were forming in the west. I needed to reach the islands before the water became dangerous. Unlike the Winnebago merchants in their big canoes, I wouldn't survive large waves. I put more muscle into my strokes and paddled on. Despite the rain clouds, visibility remained good. I didn't know if it was my imagination or wishful thinking, but I thought I saw the islands in the distance. It appeared unlikely I would arrive at the islands before the storm. I could follow the contour of the shoreline which would be safest, or I could head across the bay toward the islands—that is if what I was seeing really were the islands. Grandfather says our eyes can play tricks on us, and we see what we want to see. But if I were to catch the merchants I needed every advantage. I pointed the canoe toward what I hoped were the islands.

When I first noticed the storm clouds low on the horizon, they appeared to be slowly moving in my direction. Now that they were higher in the sky they were approaching more quickly. There must have been rain falling between what I hoped were the islands and me as I would occasionally lose sight of the islands. I had yet to experience any rain, but the waves were increasing.

I was beginning to regret my decision. Mother sent me to rescue her daughter. Now she may also be losing a son. When I lost sight of the islands I tried to visualize where they would be, but the entire western horizon was becoming obscured by a gray film. I could paddle south toward shore, but I no longer knew if the southern shore was any closer than the islands to the west. I paddled on.

One wave breached over the bow of my canoe. I took in little water, but there would be other waves, and I wouldn't always be so lucky. I shuffled my body backward. The change in the position of my weight tipped the front of the canoe upward. I could now cut through taller waves. Fortunately, I was paddling into the wind. The waves were perpendicular to my canoe. If one of those tall waves were to hit the side of my canoe, I would surely capsize. I was a good swimmer, but no one could swim far in these waves. I paddled on.

The rain was now coming down hard. My clothing was soaked. If I had not been working so hard, I would have been cold. I could see no more than fifty paces in any direction. Hopefully, I was still going west. When in doubt, I paddled into the wind. Occasionally, a flash of lightning illuminated the sky. The islands appeared larger, although I wasn't sure that I was not seeing low-lying clouds. Grandfather says it is not wise to be on a lake during a lightning storm. I had already decided what I was doing was not wise. The intense rain turned everything gray. The wind had been coming from the west. I continued paddling into the wind. Another wave breached the front of my canoe. My moose skin kneeling pad soaked up some of the water. The rest of the water sloshed around the bottom of my canoe. Another large wave and my canoe would be swamped. I paddled on. A continuous roar of water hitting rocks gradually replaced the intermittent whistle of the wind across the waves. I was getting close to the islands. Waves were no longer coming from the west. Now they were smaller, but they were coming at me from all directions. A large bolt of lightning illuminated a large sandstone cliff fifty paces in front of me, confirming my suspicions. I had reached the shelter of the islands. I dragged my paddle on the left side and the canoe turned toward shore.

I passed several more islands before I reached the southern shore. I paddled along the shore until I came to a small protective cove lined with wigwams. I pulled up to the sandy beach. A small boy who was watching me pull the canoe to shore gladly directed me to the wigwam of my cousin. If felt good to get out of the rain.

Chapter Five

"Chogan, what are you doing here?"

Aranck gave me a big bear hug, squeezing water from my wet clothing. Aranck had seen eight more winters than I had and now had a wife and wigwam of his own. He was one of my favorite cousins although two winters had passed since we last sat around the same campfire. He had grown in that time. I am sure I had also.

"I was paddling past your village and thought I would stop and say hello." I was sure my attempt at levity fell short. Proper etiquette required small talk before any discussion of important matters, but I was both physically and mentally exhausted. I would have been happy with just a dry place to sleep.

"I'm sure you heard that I had married," Aranck said. "Let me introduce you to Hurit."

Hurit was younger than Aranck but appeared mature for her age. She was almost as tall as Aranck and had long, black braids that reached down to her hips. Hurit and I exchanged pleasantries. I inquired about the health of her parents as was our custom. She was humble, yet charming, an easy person to like. Aranck had made an excellent choice for his wife, but it was not Hurit who held my attention. Hurit was holding a young infant. This news of the new-born had not yet spread to our village.

"It's a boy," Hurit said. "Would you like to hold him?"

Hurit passed the young infant to me. I liked infants. Someday I hoped to have one of my own. The baby couldn't have been more than a month or two old. I extended my index finger and the baby wrapped its little fingers around it. The infant stared into my eyes as if he could see my sole. Infants are helpless, yet so much in command. I played with the baby and then returned it to its mother when it began to cry.

"Did you come by yourself?" Aranck asked.

I'm sure my appearance during a major storm piqued Aranck's curiosity, but he was too polite to inquire. It was also unusual for someone to travel this distance alone. Any sane person would have beached the canoe long before the storm hit.

"I am honored to see you and meet your wife and new child, but I did not come for pleasure," I replied. I told Aranck about Kanti and the Winnebago merchants. He listened respectfully. I could see the concern on his face.

"The merchants briefly stopped and then left shortly before the storm," Aranck said. "One of the merchants broke his arm. They dropped him off here, so he could return home by land. He couldn't paddle a canoe and was of no further use to the other merchants."

"They must be waiting out the storm on shore or on one of the islands just as I am." I was beginning to feel more optimistic. I needed to overtake them before they disappeared into the woods at the end of the lake.

"We have an extra sleeping bench in our wigwam," Aranck said. "You are welcome to stay as long as you wish. I'm assuming you are tired from your journey."

I was more than tired. Hurit had been drying my moose-skin sleeping blanket by the fire as Aranck and I talked. Steam was no longer rising from the fur. I assumed it was now dry. I thanked Hurit and wrapped myself in the blanket. I was asleep moments after reclining on the sleeping bench.

When I awoke Aranck was adding sticks to the small fire in the center of the wigwam to take the chill out of the air. I could see sunshine through the open wigwam door. The storm had passed.

"Has it been daylight long?" I asked. I didn't want to get any farther behind the Winnebago merchants.

"You arose with the sun," Aranck replied. "Come, Hurit has prepared something to eat."

I couldn't see Hurit anywhere, but she left a large bowl of rice with chunks of muskrat for Aranck and me to share. I ate quickly. Aranck ate much slower—he was holding his son in his left arm. Fatherhood had its drawbacks.

"Don't eat so quickly," Aranck said. "You must not leave before Hurit returns."

I knew I was being rude. I good guest would enjoy the food and exchange pleasantries while eating. I was taking advantage of Aranck's food and lodging without showing any gratitude. I was hoping he could appreciate the gravity of my situation and overlook my rudeness. I was just finishing my meal when Hurit returned. She was carrying a heavy woven basket.

"I talked to many women of the village while you slept," she said. "Here is a basket of dried meat and pemmican for your journey. You must now go swiftly. I have yet to meet Kanti. I expect you to introduce her on your return trip."

***

You will be reading a lot about pemmican. If you don't remember what pemmican is or how it was made, you may want to review Chogan's website from Chogan and the Sioux Warrior found at: http://the-sioux-warrior.com/pemmican/index.html

***

Aranck and Hurit walked me down to the canoe. I offered to carry the woven bag of food, but Hurit insisted that she carry it. She carefully loaded it in the front of my canoe. Aranck had chosen a thoughtful wife. I gave Aranck a parting hug. This time my clothes were dry.

"If Grandfather and our cousin Hassun pass this way tell them I will be marking the trail. I won't return until I find Kanti." I pushed the canoe into the surf.

Aranck had provided instructions on finding the most likely inland trail that the Winnebago merchants would take on their journey to the land with no trees. It consisted of many lakes connected by portages. Unfortunately, there were several passages west. I had to find the correct one. I needed to catch them before they left Gitche Gumee. According to Aranck the far end of the lake was less than a half day away. I had plenty of food. If I were lucky, the merchants might stop to forage for food. Finding food along the way was not a difficult task, but it could slow them down enough for me to overtake them. I put all I had into my strokes. If the end of the lake was no more than a half a day away, I didn't have to pace myself.

The sun was at my back, and I didn't have to squint into the bright light. With the day being clear, I should be able to see the merchants if I got close. My muscles ached with pain, but I pushed forward. By mid-day I could see land in the west; I was approaching the western shore of Gitche Gumee. I still couldn't see any canoes. I was wondering if I would have to accept defeat. It was possible I would never see Kanti again. I added more power to my strokes. I wasn't sure I could return to my village if I didn't find Kanti. My shame would be unbearable.

When I reached the western shore I turned north. Aranck said the most probable trail was at the mouth of a small river. The river was too shallow for even small canoes such as mine, but a short portage inland led to a chain of lakes that provided passage further west. To avoid submerged rocks I maintained a distance of one hundred paces from shore.

I had not gone far when I saw a man in the distance, but there was no canoes. The man appeared to be busy with some project that was not discernable from that distance. He was most likely a hunter from one of the local villages. I was looking for men with canoes, not Ojibway hunters. But the man may have seen the Winnebago merchants pass his way. I paddled with increased effort. As the distance decreased I was able to see his clothing. He wasn't an Ojibway hunter. His clothing was that of the Winnebago! This lifted my spirits, but I would have felt better if there were several men with canoes. I saw no evidence of a young girl.

I pulled my canoe up to the beach. The man lifted his head and looked in my direction. It was Nawkaw's father. "Good morning, Chogan," he said.

I was surprised he remembered my name. We had not been formally introduced. He continued with his work as if my arrival was an expected occurrence. Many bags of merchandize were lying on the sandy beach. Nawkaw's father was loading them on a travois, which is nothing more than animal skins stretched between two poles. One person can carry large loads by pulling one end of the poles and letting the other ends drag on the ground.

***

Native Americans did not have carts with wheels like Europeans. They used travois to move heavy supplies. You will see travois used many times during Chogan's travels. To find out more about travois, see Chogan's web page at: http://winnebago-merchant.com/travois.htm

***

"Is Kanti with you?" I asked.

"She is but a short walk from here—at a lake. Nawkaw is watching her. She is quite safe. Let me finish binding this second travois, and then I will take you to her." Nawkaw's father finished binding the second travois while I watched. "One of our men broke his arm, and we had to send him home. Being short a man has slowed us down," Nawkaw's father said. "I'll send a man back for the other travois. Follow me."

The man headed into the woods dragging one of the travois. I grabbed the other travois and followed him. It was a well-marked trail. All the vegetation had been destroyed by excessive use leaving a clear path, but there were many exposed tree roots that made walking difficult. The man said it would be a short distance, but the muscles in my arms quickly began to burn. No one asked me to drag the travois, but I couldn't quit. I didn't want to admit defeat. I paused momentarily for a rest.

There was a short piece of rope strapped to the travois. I tied one end to the handle of a pole and looped the rope over my shoulders and then tied the other end to the opposite pole. I then placed my leather pouch under the rope behind my neck. I stood up. The weight was now evenly distributed over my shoulders, and the leather pouch prevented the rope from biting into my neck. I quickly caught up with Nawkaw's father.

Our path weaved around large boulders and tall trees, but for the most part we continued our westward journey. We finally came to a clearing at the edge of a lake. The four large canoes belonging to the Winnebago merchants waited patiently at the water's edge. Several men were busy loading the canoes. I looked around searching for Kanti. She was sitting on a small boulder talking to Nawkaw. I was feeling both anger and relief. Her selfish actions had created emotional pain and worry, not only for me but also for Mother.

"Kanti, I've come to take you home."

"Chogan, you made it," Kanti replied. "I was beginning to worry." Kanti's remark made little sense. She was the one who had caused others to worry.

"We need to leave now," I repeated. If we left now we might sleep in our cousin's wigwam by nightfall.

"We can't leave until all the canoes are loaded," Kanti said.

"What are you talking about? We need to start for home."

"We aren't going home," Kanti replied. "We're going to save Takoda. I traded my fish net for passage to the land with no trees. Last night I had another dream. Takoda was calling me from the rabbit hole. That means he's still alive. We're not too late."

Nawkaw's father must have heard our discussion. He had been loading the canoes with the remaining merchandise. "Kanti is free to return with you if she so wishes," he said. "She gave us a fine fish net for transportation to the land with no trees. If she still wants to go with us, that is also acceptable."

"I will be going with you," Kanti replied. "Can Chogan come with us?"

No one was asking my opinion. It was as if I were not present. If Kanti was not willing to return with me, I wasn't sure I could force her. She had made strong friendships with the Winnebago merchants. That was not surprising. Given sufficient time, she could make friends with an angry skunk.

Nawkaw's father finally turned to address me. "Chogan, you did a man's work when you dragged the travois loaded with merchandise. We lost a crew member because of a broken arm. We would be honored to have you replace him."

"He'll do it," Kanti said. The merchant walked off leaving me wondering what just happened. I had come to take Kanti home and now everyone was assuming I was joining the team.

"Kanti, Mother is expecting me to bring you home. We can't ignore her wishes."

"You've always dreamed about going to the land with no trees," Kanti said. "You want to see those purple hills that reach up to kiss the sky as much as I do. Chogan, this is our chance. We may never get another opportunity."

There was much truth to what Kanti was saying. I had wanted to see those purple hills ever since Grandfather first described them to me. And I wanted to see those shaggy deer that covered the land as far as one could see, even if only their front half was shaggy.

"What about Mother? She will now be worried about both of us."

"I have given that some thought," Kanti replied. "Despite what you are thinking, I didn't do what I did impulsively. I knew you would follow me. In two days we will arrive at a village where we have a cousin. We will have him send a message to Aranck. Aranck can send a message to Grandfather and Mother letting them know we are together and traveling to the land with no trees. There are always people traveling between the villages. I am sure Grandfather and maybe Hassun will come to help us return home.

Kanti didn't leave me with much choice. She was too big to drag back to our village, and I couldn't return without her. Mother had many friends who would care for her if Grandfather were to follow us, as I knew he would. I wouldn't admit it to anyone, but the proposed adventure was filling me with excitement. I took out my bone knife and carved our flying eagle symbol on a nearby tree. I wanted Grandfather to know we had been here.

"Will we travel in Nawkaw's father's canoe?"

"His name is Chaschunka, which is Winnebago for wave, but everyone calls him Chunka," Kanti said. "He is very nice. I'm sure you will like him. His partner broke his arm when he fell from a tree while gathering honey, so I assume we will be in his canoe. Come on." Kanti dragged me over to where Chunka was loading his canoe.

"Chogan has decided to accept your offer," Kanti said. I don't know why she had to speak for me. I was the older sibling. Chunka nodded.

"The next few days will be easy," Chunka said. "We will follow a chain of lakes. The portages will be few and short. As the trees disappear so will the lakes. Then we must drag our merchandise through deep grass. The land will be flat, but it will still be hard work. When we reach a great river we will again proceed in canoes. Trading merchandise is not an easy task."

I was strong for my age and didn't shirk from work. I assumed I could work as hard as Nawkaw. "I brought some food," I said. I held up my bag of pemmican. "I am also good with a bow."

"We share all food," Chunka said. "We will quickly discover your expertise with the bow, as we will have to forage along the way."

I assumed my employment had begun. I grabbed a bag of merchandise and began loading the canoe. I had rarely seen such large canoes, and I had never ridden in one. They looked like they would be impossible to steer. That task would no doubt fall to Chunka. When the four canoes were loaded, Kanti and I climbed aboard. We knelt near the front of the canoe. It was wide enough for the two of us to kneel side by side. Chunka and Nawkaw knelt in the back of the canoe after they pushed us into the lake. Supplies and merchandise filled the middle of the canoe.

We were in the first of the four canoes, since they assumed our canoe would be the slowest. This assumption was not without merit. Nawkaw and I were not yet grown men and Kanti's contribution was limited.

The canoes moved remarkably well for their great size. I couldn't see how Chunka was guiding our canoe. I assumed it was a joint venture between Chunka and Nawkaw. I had been paddling non-stop for two days. My arms were tired, but I vowed not to let our canoe lag behind the other three. Our journey had begun.

Chapter Six

"Why are we stopping?"

One of the canoes was paddling toward shore. We recently stopped for a break. Another break so close to the first one was unusual. It was the afternoon of the third day, and I was tired. A break for any reason was welcome. Chunka conferred with the other merchants in his native tongue. I didn't understand what was said, but it was obvious the Winnebago merchants were not happy.

"One of the canoes sprang a leak," Chunka said, replying to my question. "A submerged boulder scrapped through the birch bark."

I was not one to enjoy someone's misfortune, but my arms and back were sore. It would take the rest of the day to make the necessary repairs. The afternoon was ours. I carved our eagle symbol on a nearby tree as was now my habit.

"Do you think Grandfather and Hassun can follow our trail?" Kanti asked. Other than our marks on trees there was nothing to follow. Canoes do not leave a trodden path, and so far the portages were limited in number.

"If anyone can follow our trail it will be Grandfather." I wished I felt as confident as I spoke.

"Chogan, I'm sorry for the trouble I've caused, but I have to do this. I had another dream last night. It was so real. Maybe it's not a rabbit hole. Maybe it is something else. But I always get stuck before I reach Takoda. It is so dark and scary. We have to save Takoda."

I didn't want to tell Kanti, but two days ago I had a dream about Takoda. He was pleading for help. I awoke feeling scared. I could remember little of the dream. Maybe the Medicine Woman was right. Takoda's spirit could be reaching out to me also. According to the Medicine Woman, as long as we continued having these dreams, Takoda was still alive. Unfortunately, we still had a long way to go.

"Kanti, I saw many deer tracks along the riverbank not far from here. I'm going to see if I can shoot one of them when they come to the river to drink. You stay here with Nawkaw."

The odds were not in my favor. I would be lucky to see any deer and bringing one down with a single arrow would be difficult, but I had nothing better to do with my afternoon. Sometimes it's nice to be alone in the woods with one's thoughts. I was getting tired of pemmican and dried meat. I longed for fresh roasted meat like Mother makes. I wondered how many full moons would pass before I would see home. Despite the lure of adventure I was getting homesick.

I crushed some grass between two stones and then smeared the green coloring over my hands and face as my cousin Hassun once taught me. Then I broke off some ferns and stuck them into my clothing. In order for my arrow to have much power I had to be close to the deer. I headed into the woods following the river. I found a spot downwind from the watering hole and sat quietly.

Many people would have found what I was doing boring. I found immense enjoyment. A chickadee scolded me from the treetops. A mallard duck was swimming around the shallows. I could have easily shot the duck, but it would not feed many men and it had a flock of ducklings circling around. Grandfather says we should never kill a mother with young. I waited.

A large snake slithered by. I hate snakes. Grandfather says some snakes have a poisonous bite. None of these snakes live along Gitche Gumee, but we were no longer along Gitche Gumee, and I had never seen such a snake before. I wondered if this snake had a poisonous bite. I waited and the snake slithered away.

I saw some movement along the riverbank. A young fawn stepped into the clearing. It would provide more meat than a duck, but Grandfather says we must let the young grow up. Soon its mother joined the fawn. She was more wary and looked around before she bent down for a drink of cool water. I waited.

A small fox and several more ducks made an appearance and left. My left leg was going to sleep. I didn't think I could sit still much longer. I was about to admit defeat and leave empty handed when I saw a bush move. It could be nothing more than a large bird jumping from branch to branch, but I decided to wait a little bit longer. The bushes stopped moving. I waited. Then a large buck stepped into the clearing. It was early in the summer and his antlers were just beginning to grow. The buck stopped and stared directly at me. I was downwind so I knew he couldn't smell me, but could he see me? I froze in place and waited. He looked at the water and then looked back at me. I was painted green and covered with branches, still I must have looked out of place. His thirst finally got the best of him. He turned away and cautiously walked toward the river's edge.

While he was not looking I notched my straightest arrow and pulled back on the bowstring. This had been Grandfather's bow and had a heavy draw. I could only hold it back for a short period before my right arm would begin to tremble. The buck was facing away from me as it drank from the river. An arrow in the butt would not bring down such a large animal. It would run a considerable distance before it dropped and died a slow death from infection. I needed to shoot the buck in the front chest or shoulder. I waited.

My arm was beginning to tremble when the buck looked up and turned slightly toward me exposing the front shoulder. Something on the far side of the river had caught his attention. He did not see the arrow coming from the strange bush that had earlier fostered his concern. He jumped into the air. A deer's back legs are powerful, but it is the front legs that guide a deer in flight. With the arrow deeply imbedded in the left shoulder, the deer fell to the ground. I was quickly upon him. I took my bone knife and cut the deer's throat. Grandfather says we must not let game suffer needlessly.

There was much excitement when I returned to camp dragging a big buck. I think everyone was as tired of dried meat and pemmican as I was. It was a lucky shot and I was fortunate that the buck happened to be thirsty. But I was standing in front of a troop of hungry Winnebago merchants. The carcass of the dead deer was their only concern. I'm sure they were all salivating over the image of a roasting deer.

"We are going to need lots of firewood," Kanti told the merchants. "And make sure it comes from trees that shed their leaves in the winter."

The merchants were not accustomed to taking orders from a woman and a very young one at that, but the order made sense and they were hungry. I can roast a piece of meat on a stick, but I had never roasted an entire deer carcass. Kanti had assisted Mother during many of our village feasts. I would have to trust her judgement. While I was skinning the deer, Kanti was searching for stout poles with a "Y" branch at the top. She found two of these and cut them at the bases with the help of Nawkaw. I was beginning to like him more each day.

"We now need a long, straight pole and it has to come from a living tree so it does not burn. Nawkaw and I dutifully followed orders. The first two we selected did not meet Kanti's high standards, although they looked good to me. She was agreeable to our third choice. Nawkaw and I took turns cutting at the pole with our knives. Nawkaw's knife was made of very sharp obsidian and cut much faster than mine. I vowed I would return home with a similar knife.

"Now cut off all the branches."

I was wondering if Nawkaw would resent Kanti giving orders, but he began cutting the branches. I assumed they had become close friends in my absence. We were about to cut the last branch when she told us to leave an arm length of branch attached to the pole. We were confused with the order but did as directed.

"Help me attach the deer to the pole," Kanti ordered.

Nawkaw and I cut off some of the sinew that ran along the back of the buck and secured the deer to the pole. In no time we had the deer roasting over hot coals.

Kanti adjusted the coals periodically with a wooden poker and added more wood as needed. She rotated the deer using the uncut branch on the roasting pole. No one challenged her judgement. They could smell the roasting meat, and that was ample reason for allowing Kanti free reign over the cooking. The Winnebago merchants gathered around the fire pit and patiently waited.

The front legs cooked faster than the rest of the deer. Kanti cut these pieces off and passed them to the Winnebago who appeared to be the leader. I was impressed with Kanti's wisdom. As the rest of the deer became fully roasted, Kanti cut off more pieces and inserted small sticks. The meat was too hot to handle. Soon every merchant was sitting around the fire eating fresh roasted venison on a stick.

Previously, Kanti and I had been treated as baggage. The merchants accepted Nawkaw only because of his father. We had no redeeming value. It was not publicly discussed, but I was sure many of the merchants questioned the wisdom of taking us with them. That all changed when I dragged the deer back to camp, and Kanti expertly roasted it over the fire. Now we were part of the team.

After four more days we ran out of lakes and rivers. We beached our canoes and transferred our baggage to travois. The weight assigned to the travois that Nawkaw and I pulled was less than that of the men, but not by much. Even Kanti who had paid for her passages was given a travois to pull. Fortunately, the land for as far as I could see, appeared flat. There were still trees, but they were limited to riverbanks. Knee high grass now covered most of the land. I was already missing the lakes and trees. I could paddle a canoe faster than I could pull a travois. I was gaining a new respect for traveling merchants.

"How much longer will we be pulling these travois?" I didn't wish to sound impatient but I was impatient. Every day the land looked the same. I was expecting something more romantic and exciting. Where were the purple hills that reached up to touch the sky?

"In less days than you have fingers on your hand we will reach a great river that will take us westward," Nawkaw replied. "It is called the Missouris which means *river of wooden canoe people*. You have traveled in canoes made from the bark of trees. We will travel upriver in canoes made from a tree without the bark."

Making a canoe from the tree and not the bark didn't make sense. Perhaps I heard wrong or Nawkaw was making a joke. I decided not to pursue the point. My arms and back were too sore to discuss such matters. I was looking forward to the end of the day.

After dragging the travois twelve days, one of the merchants called for a halt. They began talking in their native tongue that neither Kanti nor I understood. Unless they were talking directly to Kanti or me, that was their behavior, which we had learned to accept. They were pointing to a brown spot in the distance.

"That's a tatanka bull," Nawkaw said. "The bull must be old or sick, as it has been deserted by the herd."

***

Chogan has finally seen his first buffalo. He will see many more before this adventure is over. To learn more about buffalo please see Chogan's buffalo web site at: http://winnebago-merchant.com/buffalo.htm

***

The merchants continued their discussion. Since they occasionally pointed toward the tatanka, I assumed the animal was somehow involved in their discussion. Then one of the men pointed to a nearby granite pillar. It appeared out of place in an otherwise sea of grass. A tall man could not reach the top, and the sides rose up almost vertically. A small flat surface adorned the top.

One of the men must have asked Nawkaw to climb to the top. Nawkaw grabbed one of the few handholds and carefully pulled himself upward. The sides of the granite pillar were not smooth, but the footholds and hand grips were small and far between. He gradually made his way to the top. For some reason, the men were not impressed. I wasn't sure I could do any better. After Nawkaw climbed down, Chunka walked over to me.

"Do you think you can climb any faster," he asked.

I assumed this was some sort of competition, although I did not understand the purpose. I grabbed a handhold and began pulling myself up. Like Nawkaw, I found most footholds and handgrips too small to be of any use. I finally worked my way to the top, but the platform was too small for my big feet and I was unable to stand at the top. I cautiously climbed back down.

"Let me show how it's done."

Kanti is more competitive than I. She assumes she can do everything I do—and better. She attacked the granite pillar like a frightened red squirrel climbing a tree. Her tiny feet and hands found foot holds and hand grips that I didn't know existed. In no time she was standing on top of the small platform, totally pleased with herself. If I had closed my eyes to sneeze I would have missed the whole thing. Kanti climbed half way down and then jumped the rest of the way.

"Can you do that again?" Chunka asked. For reasons unknown to me, the Winnebago merchants were impressed with Kanti's climbing skills. Without offering a reply to Chunka's question, Kanti scampered back to the top. She was even faster and more sure-footed than the time before.

The merchants again conferred in their own language. I couldn't understand what they were saying, but from their gestures I assumed it had something to do with the tatanka bull out in the field and the granite pillar. It made no logical sense, but climbing the pillar was a part of their strategy. Whatever it was, it provided a break in our walk. Kanti and I sat in the shade of the granite pillar and waited. The distant tatanka bull continued eating the grass.

"We need to talk," Chunka said in our language. "We are getting low on food and that tatanka bull could provide meat for many days, perhaps for the rest of our journey."

"Will you spear it?" I asked. "I don't think one of my arrows will do much more that anger such a large animal."

"We can bring it down with a couple of well-placed spears if we get close enough, but the tatanka are very fast," Chunka said. "We can't get close without trickery."

I assumed climbing the rock was part of the trickery, but I failed to see how the granite pillar would trick any animal into a piece of meat roasting over a fire. I waited for Chunka to explain.

"We can hide two men with spears in the grass on either side of the stone. The rest of us will walk around behind the tatanka. If we walk slowly the tatanka will not spook and run away. We can gradually encourage it to walk toward this stone." Chunka pointed to the large boulder behind us. "Getting the tatanka near the stone will not be adequate. We need to get it right next to the stone—and distracted."

I assumed this was the part where Kanti and I were to assist, although I didn't know how. Neither of us had experience hunting tatankas.

"Kanti, you don't have to do this," Chunka said, "but if you were to hide in the tall grass in front of the stone until the tatanka got close and then stood up and threw stones at the animal he might run away. Then we have no fresh meat to eat. It is also likely that you may make the tatanka angry. Lone bull tatankas tend to be irritable, and an angry tatanka can be very dangerous. If it charges at you, you will have to climb to safety on the granite pillar. While you are distracting the tatanka the two men hiding in the tall grass can rise up and spear it in the shoulders."

"I don't think Kanti…"

"I'll do it."

"As I said, this could be dangerous."

"I always wanted to see a tatanka up close," Kanti said.

"You could trip and fall," I said.

"I said I will do it." Kanti glared at me with her hands on her hips. It was the typical stance she used when no amount of logic would sway her mind.

"If Kanti has problems the men with spears will try to divert the bull," Chunka said.

I wasn't convinced by the "try" part of Chunka's reassurance. Any number of things could go wrong. I didn't know much about tatankas, but they were big and looked mean. It was my job to protect my little sister. It would be easier if she were to help me.

Chunka directed the men to encircle the bull. We moved slowly to avoid spooking the beast. I looked back at the stone and could see neither Kanti nor the two men with spears. They were well hidden in the deep grass. Once we had encircled the tatanka we slowly walked forward. The bull looked up and walked away from us. He was moving toward the protruding stone as Chunka had hoped. He was also moving toward Kanti. I have been on several deer hunts with our villagers, but we never used a child for bait.

We continued our slow march. Our circle became smaller. The bull showed no fear of us, but it didn't wish to get too close to us either. It slowly walked toward the stone. It was fifty paces from the stone and nothing happened. I mentally begged Kanti to stand up and throw her stones at the beast and then run for the safety of the stone pillar. The tatanka was now thirty paces from the stone. I wondered if Kanti and the two men with spears were still there. We move closer to the bull. The tatanka looked nothing like a shaggy deer except for the front half. Its legs were shorter than a deer or moose, and its head was big and ugly. There was almost no neck.

When the bull was twenty paces from the stone Kanti stood up. She looked so small next to the Tatanka. I wanted to yell to her and tell her to run for the stone. Kanti not only stood her ground but she threw some rocks at the beast. Even from my distance I could hear the animal snort. It was not a happy snort. The bull began pawing the ground. I assumed that was also not a friendly gesture. Kanti threw another stone hitting the tatanka on the nose. The bull lowered its massive head and charged toward Kanti.

If I had blinked I would have missed it. Kanti spun around and raced for the stone. When she was still a pace away she leaped into the air and landed midway up the pillar. In no time she was standing on top glaring down at the snorting beast below her. She yelled at the Tatanka to keep its attention. I don't think Mother would have approved of some of the words she used, but it seemed to work. The bull was so enraged at Kanti that it didn't notice as two men with spears rushed at it from both sides. They stabbed their spears into the front shoulders and then ran for cover behind the stone. It wasn't necessary. The tatanka immediately fell to its knees. Everyone rushed in to complete the kill. Kanti climbed down to a hero's welcome.

I could now look at a tatanka up close. Other than the shaggy front half it looked nothing like a shaggy deer, although I could come up with no better description. It had a very ugly head and the strangest antlers. Instead of branching like deer antlers they were thick at the base and then narrowed to a point. Nawkaw said the antlers don't fall off in the spring like deer antlers and both male and female tatanka have them. Ugly as it was, the tatanka was a noble beast and I felt sad, but I also felt hungry. I assumed there would be another big feast with all the roast meat I could eat. The men were already skinning the animal.

"We need to build a fire," Nawkaw said. I looked around, but saw no firewood.

"Where are we going to get firewood?" I asked. Nawkaw bent down and picked up a flat circular object. I looked around and found several similar objects.

"This is tatanka dung," Nawkaw said. "It's dried poop and burns quite well."

When I began parting the grass, I discovered the dung was everywhere. There must have been a large herd of tatanka in this area in the recent past. So many animals in such a small space was beyond my imagination. I have seen five or six deer congregate, but their droppings were insignificant.

It didn't take Kanti and Nawkaw long to gather an armful of dung. I was carrying such a large pile that I had to look around the stack I was carrying to see where I was going. We dumped the dung beside a small fire one of the men had started.

"We'll stay here until morning, so we can dry the meat," Chunka said. "It'll provide sufficient food for us to reach the river."

There was lots of meat but not an unlimited supply. It provided hope that the river was no more than a few days away. I prefer water travel to walking. I knew the purple hills that reached up to kiss the sky were far from my home, but we had already traveled forever and the purple hills didn't appear any closer.

Kanti and I took our bone knives and began cutting meat into thin ribbons. We hung the meat over the poles from our travois, which the merchants had fashioned into drying racks. Then we extended the fire into a strip in front of the drying rack. By evening we had the carcass stripped of meat. Everyone reserved a large piece of meat for our evening meal, which we roasted at the end of long sticks. The merchants reserved the heart for Kanti. The merchants considered Kanti the hero of the day.

We sat around the campfire of dung and watched the sun set in the west. The Winnebago merchants talked and laughed in their own language. I could tell by their gestures they were discussing Kanti's roll in killing the tatanka. She would remain a hero. I had to admit I was proud of her although I still didn't think it was a wise decision. The tatanka was a large animal, and it was angry.

The sky darkened revealing more stars than I had ever seen. At home I could look out over a lake and see half of the sky. Now I could see stars from one horizon to the next.

"Do you think Grandfather is seeing the same stars?" Kanti asked.

She had also been looking at the stars. Perhaps she was getting homesick. I wondered if she was now having misgivings about her decision to save Takoda—assuming Takoda needed saving. Her decision impacted Mother, Grandfather, and me. It would have been more prudent if Kanti had discussed her decision with us before she left.

"If the sky is clear and he is looking up, he will see the same stars." I said. "The sky may be obscured with trees. I don't know how far he is behind us. I've been marking our trail as we go, but tracking a person is always tedious and slow."

"Do you realy think Grandfather is following us?"

"He will be following us, but he may not have left until three days after we left," I said.

"Will he be angry with me?"

"Probably, but he cares about you," I said. "If Takoda is in trouble and we can help him, Grandfather will understand."

"Do you think Takoda is in trouble?" Kanti asked. "There are days when I have doubts, but I'm still having those dreams."

"Kanti, I wasn't going to tell you, but I have also had dreams. Takoda is moaning and crying out for help, but I always awaken. There are never any details, no rabbit holes. We must get to sleep. Tomorrow will be another strenuous day." All the merchants were sleeping. I rolled up in my sleeping blanket and quickly fell sleep under a brilliant display of stars.

Chapter Seven

"Nawkaw, I thought you said the river was right around the corner."

It was a bit of a joke, but no one was laughing. We had been walking a straight line for days dragging our travois behind us. We were already in the land with no trees. If I strained my eyes I might see a tree or two in the distance. They congregated about small streams, streams that were too small to navigate. Without trees there was no shade. I gained a new respect for the sun's heat. We passed several tatanka herds that must have numbered in the hundreds. Nawkaw said they were small herds. They looked big to me. One such herd could feed my entire village for several winters. We gave the tatanka a wide berth and they ignored us. We had plenty of dried meat, and they outnumbered us.

"It is just beyond the next hill," Nawkaw replied.

That was another standard joke that had lost its amusement. I had never seen such flat land. If I were to stand on tatanka dung piled three high and gaze into the west, I had little doubt I would be able to see the sun rising in the east. It was the constant banter with Nawkaw that kept my spirits high. I had gained a new respect for traveling merchants.

"It really isn't much farther," Chunka said. "It wouldn't surprise me if we camped beside the Missouris River tonight."

Chunka's comment must have inspired everyone as the pace quickened. I was not the only one who was tired of dragging a travois through the hot sun. When the sun was high in the sky we stopped at a small stream to fill our containers with water. I never considered water as a precious commodity, but I have since changed my mind. Water in the land with no trees can be difficult to find. Nawkaw said people often die from thirst. That would never happen in the land where I lived. We drank our fill and then filled several tatanka stomachs with water.

"We won't need to fill all our containers," Chunka said. "This stream spills into the Missouris River. We will follow it and replenish our water as needed."

Less water containers meant less weight to carry. We set off again on foot. We didn't closely follow the stream that wound its way through the land like a snake. We always knew it was there. The water-seeking bushes were a dead giveaway. The sun was sinking low in the sky when I first saw the row of trees in the distance. These were not mere bushes but tall trees.

"That's the big river," Chunka said. "We will sleep there tonight and tomorrow we will follow the river west until we arrive at a Mandan village. They will provide canoes for the rest of the trip west."

The trees were farther from us than they first appeared, but we reached the riverbank while there was still daylight. We had seen only small streams since we left the woodlands. I was expecting a large stream but still small by my standards. I was unprepared for what I saw. The river was larger than any river I had ever seen, even during a flood. We set our travois down and looked out at the river—it was our gateway to the west. It looked like it could take us far. The only downside was that we would be paddling upstream. Chunka gave everyone some dried meat. We ate in silence and then rolled up in our sleeping blankets and fell asleep. It had been a long day.

I awoke the following morning with the sun in my eyes. Chunka was already up and about. Kanti, who awakes with the birds, said he sent a runner to the Mandan village. That made little sense. Now we were short one person. That meant more weight on the remaining travois. We ate some pemmican and dried meat for breakfast and set about loading our travois. Chunka was in no hurry. This was unusual for him.

"Who's going to carry the extra supplies?" I asked Nawkaw. "I don't think I can carry more than I am."

"You will be pleasantly surprised," he said. He smiled but offered no further explanation. I rolled up my sleeping blanket and tied it to my travois. I waited until Kanti was finished rolling up her sleeping blanket.

"Kanti, I need to talk to you." I led Kanti toward a tree where no one could hear us.

"Are you okay?" she asked when we were beyond the hearing of others. She must have seen the concern on my face.

"I had a dream last night," I said. "Takoda was calling to me from a distance. He sounded like he was in pain, but I couldn't see him. Someone was telling me I had to help him. I heard you talking, but I can no longer remember what you said in the dream. This is the second night I've had such a dream."

"I'm also having dreams," Kanti replied. "There is still a rabbit hole and I still get stuck, but Takoda's voice is louder. Chogan I think Takoda's spirit is gaining strength as we get closer to Takoda. I just hope we don't arrive too late."

"The Medicine Woman said we can assume Takoda is still alive as long as we have these dreams."

I had assumed Kanti's dreams were just dreams. I was beginning to wonder now that I was having similar dreams. Takoda was a good friend. If he were in need and we could help, the trip and hardships would be worth it. I wasn't sure Mother and Grandfather would agree. Grandfather will be angry. I would offer Kanti my support when Grandfather arrived. There were many times when I could have forced Kanti to return. Perhaps I was supportive from the beginning. Deep inside I knew I wanted to see those purple hills that Grandfather always talked about.

When Kanti and I returned to the group several men in strange clothing were jubilantly talking to the Winnebago merchants as if they were long lost friends. I assumed they were from the Mandan village. The runner had not been gone long, so their village must be nearby.

I picked up the two poles of my travois, but was pushed aside by two Mandan men. Each man grabbed a pole and almost ran toward their village. I should not have been surprised. We were just as excited when the Winnebago merchants arrived at our village. Kanti and I followed the crowd toward the Mandan village.

The village sat on the bank of the Missouris River. The lodges within the village were surrounded by a palisade of pointed timbers taller than two men. A deep ditch in front of the palisade added more security. The Mandan were friendly, but I got the impression not all Indian tribes lived peacefully.

The lodges inside the wooden palisade were unlike anything I had previously seen. They were large earthen domes with an entrance made of wood posts and crossbeams that created a small tunnel. The inside of the lodges was spacious but otherwise similar to a wigwam except the walls were made from wooden poles, not birch bark. Instead of sleeping benches, they had raised rectangular bedframes with animal skins stretched across the frame. These beds were fully enclosed for privacy or for protection from insects. We never had such privacy in our wigwams. With so few trees I wondered where they found the wood. There were a few trees growing along the river, but that source appeared limited. An opening at the top of the lodge expelled the smoke from the cooking fire located in the center of the lodge.

I wanted to explore more, but I was employed by the Winnebago merchants, and they were about to conduct business. I helped the merchants lay out their goods like they did in our village, but instead of displaying obsidian and other rocks found in this area they produced clam shells and shells from a variety of snails that had been crafted into necklaces. Such items were so abundant along the shore of Gitche Gumee that it was difficult to believe their value here.

***

The Mandan were river people with villages along the Missouri River in what is now North and South Dakota. They spoke the Siouan language similar to the

Winnebagos. You can read more about them at: http://winnebago-merchant.com/Mandan.htm
***

What I found most fascinating were the people. Some of them had eyes that were blue like the sky on a clear day, and their hair was the color of dry grass. These people were few in number, but difficult to overlook. I tried not to stare. Grandfather says it is not polite to stare.

Kanti and I couldn't speak their language, but we stood behind Chunka's merchandise and tried to be helpful. We showed the snail-shell necklaces and other trinkets to customers. They would say something and we would nod. We left the actual trading to Chunka.

I awoke the following morning thinking it would be another day of trading, but I found Chunka packing his merchandise into thatched baskets.

"Are we leaving today?" I asked.

"We are traveling west to visit another Mandan village," he replied.

I was hoping for another day of rest. Pulling a travois is hard on the back and shoulders. Chunka traded some of the merchandise from my travois, which should have made it easier to drag. There was no guarantee that the merchandise he received in trade was any lighter. I began to prepare my travois for the journey. I had learned it was best to have the heavy items closer to the ground.

"You won't need that," Chunka said. "We're traveling by canoe."

I nodded, trying to appear indifferent, but my heart was leaping with joy. I loved canoeing.

"I assume you and Kanti can handle a canoe on your own," he said. "These are smaller canoes, made for two people, but they still carry a lot of supplies."

I followed Chunka down to the river. I had traveled in many canoes, most of them made from birch bark, but occasionally from elm bark. These canoes had no bark at all. They were tree trunks with the centers cut out. The canoes looked heavy, and I questioned if they would float.

"This will be your canoe," Chunka said. "Nawkaw and I will be in the lead canoe, and you and Kanti will follow behind us."

Kanti examined our canoe with a skeptical eye. I was sure she shared my concerns. Neither of us had paddled a log before.

"They handle better than they look," Chunka said. "Birch trees are nice, but they are a long way from here. Paddle these canoes like any other canoe and you will do fine."

I wanted adventure. Now I was getting it whether I wanted it or not. We loaded our personal belongings and then filled our canoe with merchandise. Chunka said we would sleep in the next village, which was upstream. The purple hills couldn't be too much farther, but the land without trees was so vast. I worried that we would never find Takoda in such a large space.

"Are you and Kanti ready to shove off?" Nawkaw asked. "Father says he will go slowly until you are comfortable with the canoe. We will stay close to shore. The current is not as swift near the shore." I nodded. Kanti and I climbed into the canoe. Several Mandan men cheerfully shoved us into the river. I began paddling.

Our Winnebago hosts had been good to us. Chunka treated us almost as a father. Still it was good to be in our own canoe where Kanti and I could talk privately. Our dreams and concerns for Takoda's safety were best not shared with others, although I think Kanti mentioned her dreams when she bartered for transportation west. I allowed our canoe to lag behind Nawkaw and Chunka's canoe until we were outside of their hearing.

"Kanti, do you have plans for finding Takoda?" I asked. "The Sioux are a mighty nation with many villages. We don't even know the name of Takoda's village."

"He told me he lived at the base of the purple hills."

"I have yet to see hills of any color," I said, "although with the haze and cloudy skies of the last few days we could walk passed the hills and not notice."

I heard Grandfather tell many times of his trip to the land of no trees. He was not much older than I. He told of the shaggy deer that covered the ground from horizon to horizon. He told of the beautiful purple hills that reached up to kiss the sky. I had seen the tatanka, but I so wanted to see those purple hills Grandfather talked about.

Grandfather made friends with a Sioux boy named Wambleeska. They taught their languages to each other. Wambleeska and Grandfather have since become great chiefs of their nations, but remain friends. Takoda was Wambleeska's grandson. The previous summer Takoda and a few teenage friends raided our village.

Fortunately, Takoda was the only person injured. An arrow hit him in the left thigh, but he escaped into the woods. He would have died if Kanti and I hadn't found him. We removed the arrow and nursed him back to health without anyone from our village knowing. Takoda learned our language from his grandfather, so we were able to communicate. Now if our dreams were correct Takoda was again in trouble, but we had no way of finding him.

"I was hoping we would receive more guidance in my dreams, but they are always the same," Kanti said. "I am stuck in a rabbit hole and Takoda keeps pleading for help."

"This river keeps going west. Sooner or later we will find the purple hills."

We arrived at another Mandan village before nightfall. It was the third Mandan village we visited. Kanti and I wandered around while the Winnebago men traded merchandise. The village was similar to the other Mandan villages. It had a wooden palisade surrounding it. We walked around the outside of the palisade and watched the Mandan working their fields. They were mostly farmers. Unlike us, their villages were permanent. They grew corn, beans and squash. It looked like a lot of work. I preferred harvesting the crops nature cultivated. Gathering wild rice in the fall was so much easier than what the Mandan farmers did for their livelihood.

The Winnebago merchants ate well when visiting the Mandan villages. That evening the Mandan treated us to a feast of fish, beans, and some of their squash. I must admit, it tasted better than steamed rice, although I would rather eat muskrat or beaver than fish. After we had eaten our fill, Chunka pulled Kanti and me aside.

"We are as far west as we will travel," Chunka said. "Tomorrow we will leave for the land of trees and water. You are welcome to return with us."

"No, we must go on." As usual, Kanti did not wait for me to reply. I nodded. I was finally in agreement with Kanti. We had to do whatever was needed to help Takoda.

"I feared you might say that. You have become as worthy to me as my own son, Nawkaw, but you are on a quest you find equally worthy, and I wish you well. I have arranged for a canoe to be available in the morning. Follow the river west and it will take you to the land of the Sioux."

"Thank you Chunka," I replied. "You have treated us as family and we are grateful, but we must find Takoda. He is also like family."

We left Chunka to search for our sleeping blankets. It would be difficult to part ways with the Winnebago. They had been good companions and spoke the language of the Sioux and many other languages. Until we found Takoda or Wambleeska, we couldn't converse with anyone. We fell asleep with heavy hearts.

I awoke with the early morning sun shining in my eyes. We had been invited to sleep as a guest in one of the earth domes, but I preferred the open air when the weather is warm. The beautiful sunrise was one of the reasons. It appeared be the beginning of a clear day. No clouds obscured the sky, but that could always change. I rolled up my sleeping blanket.

"Chogan!" Kanti was facing west, ignoring the beautiful sunrise. "Look behind you."

I turned to see what had so impressed Kanti. If Kanti had described it, I would not have believed her. There before us were the purple hills. They reached high into the heavens. I could see how they could have impressed Grandfather.

"They are still far away," Nawkaw said. I had been so fascinated with the purple hills that I didn't see him walk up to us.

"How does one begin to describe them?" I asked.

"You don't," he replied. "You must experience them. I have never been to the top of those hills, but I have been told the white on the taller peaks is snow."

It was summer. I found it difficult to believe there would be snow anywhere. This view alone was worth any hardships we had experience in the past or might experience in the future.

"My father says we will be departing. I've made this trip several times. You and Kanti have made it much more enjoyable. If you seek the Sioux follow the Missouris River. It will lead you west toward the purple hills. It will be difficult, since few Sioux speak your language. Hopefully, you will find your friend who can speak for you."

"Thank you, Nawkaw."

We found Chunka by the water's edge. He and the other Winnebago merchants were loading their canoes for the return trip. I notice one canoe was empty except for a generous supply of food. I assumed it was ours.

"It is not too late to change your mind," Chunka said.

"Thank you, but we must go on." For once Kanti allowed me to speak. She knew what I would say.

"I knew you would say that. We have left provisions in your canoe. They will last many days. Follow the Missouris and it will take you west to the purple hills."

"How can we find the Sioux?" I asked.

"You will not find them. They will find you. That part scares me. The Sioux and the Ojibway do not always live peacefully."

I nodded. That also scared me. We first met Takoda when he and a bunch of teenagers attacked our village. It was only through extraordinary luck and effort that

Takoda, Kanti, and I were able to prevent all-out war between the two mighty nations.

"We must be going," I said. "We thank you again." I nodded toward Chunka as a respectful gesture and then headed toward our canoe. Nawkaw was standing beside the canoe. Nawkaw had been a great friend during our trip. We would miss him.

"You will soon be in the land of the Sioux Nation. When you first meet the Sioux people place your bow and spear on the ground as a gesture of peace. You will be outnumbered and you will be on their land. If you are lucky, they will see it as a gesture of friendship."

"Thank you, Nawkaw, for all your help."

"I should be thanking you and Kanti. I seldom travel with anyone my age. You made the trip more pleasant," Nawkaw replied. "I will never forget Kanti and the tatanka. I have never seen anyone move so quickly. I didn't want to say so because we truly needed the meat, but I feared for her life. She ran like an antelope, leaped like a jackrabbit, and climbed like a red squirrel. I will be telling that story around campfires until I am an old man."

Kanti climbed into the front of canoe, and I climbed into the rear of the canoe. Nawkaw pushed us into the river. We were on our own.

Chapter Eight

"I don't see how those purple hills can get much higher," Kanti said.

We had been paddling toward them for the last five days. The hills kept getting larger, but we never seemed to get closer. The sun now set when the day was little more than half gone. We had to be in Takoda's homeland, but we hadn't seen any Sioux.

"It is getting late," I said. "Let's pull over to that sandbar on your right."

That was for information only. Kanti had no control of the canoe. That was reserved for the paddler in the rear. I dragged my paddle in the water on the right side and the canoe slowly turned in that direction. If this had been a birch bark canoe we could have made the turn in less than a canoe's length. With the heavy wooden canoe, we had to plan turns in advance.

The canoe plowed into the soft sand at the river's edge. Kanti and I got out and tried to pull the canoe farther onto the sand. With a birch bark canoe we could have carried the entire canoe onto the beach. The wooden canoe was not only heavy, but offered few handholds to assist pulling the canoe onto the sand. We left our paddles in the canoe and carried our sleeping skins to the grassy area above the river.

"Look, Chogan, there are those funny animals again. I'm going to spear a couple of them for dinner while you create a fire."

Kanti had returned to her habit of directing my life. When the Winnebago were present, she had been more reserved. That was now changing. I wasn't optimistic about Kanti spearing one of those animals, but the nights had been cool and we needed a fire.

We had seen the noisy animals many times in the distance, but now the little brown rodents surrounded us. They looked like the ground hogs we had back home. I would have enjoyed their company if not for the constant noise. They sounded like barking dogs when disturbed, which was all the time now that Kanti and I had arrived. There must have been hundreds of them in this underground colony. Kanti placed her spear tip at the entrance of a burrow into which one of the animals had scampered. I wouldn't have that much patience, but Kanti waited for the animal to pop up its head.

I gathered tatanka dung for our fire. It was everywhere as were the tatanka. I saw a brown mass in the distance that had to be a herd of tatanka. They would not be feeding us during the rest of our trip.

"Got one!"

Kanti held up her spear with a wiggling animal impaled on its tip. Maybe they would be easier to hunt than I had expected. I got out my board and spindle to start the fire. I was sure the animals would taste better cooked. I had a small fire going and had not yet skinned the first animal when Kanti brought in a second animal;

we would each have an entire animal for dinner. The animals were small, but they were real food. I was getting tired of the dried beans and corn the Mandan had given us. Kanti and I found green sticks growing near the river and roasted our animals over a tatanka dung fire. We sat in the shade of the purple hills and ate our fill. Then we spread out our sleeping blankets and rolled up in them near our fire. Sleep came quickly.

I awoke with Kanti's spear poking me in the ribs; at least I thought it was her spear. I opened my eyes to discover a large man sticking me with his spear—and it was not the blunt end. I looked around. There were five men and a large dog. One of men was holding my bow and quiver.

"Kanti, wake up."

Kanti is always spontaneous and impulsive. She acts before she thinks. Instead of submitting to the obvious. She grabbed her spear and jumped up. She stood defiantly pointing her spear at the five armed men. The men had assumed a ten-year-old girl would not be armed and did not bother searching for her weapon. Apparently, young girls in the Sioux Nation didn't carry weapons. Neither did young girls in the Ojibway Nation—except for Kanti!

"Lay down your spear."

Kanti aggressively pointed her spear at one Sioux warrior and then another. The Sioux warriors looked at each other, trying to decide if they should spear her or spank her.

Kanti, lay your spear on the ground. Remember what Nawkaw said!"

I didn't know if Kanti was listening to me or had finally come to her senses and decided she couldn't change the outcome of our encounter. We were prisoners and at the mercy of the five Sioux men.

I stood up and gradually shuffled my way over to Kanti with my empty hands in the open. The five men began to argue. I couldn't understand their language, but I assumed they were discussing our fate. A young man with a large scar on his face did most of the talking, and he seemed angry. I didn't know what their mission for the day was, but we were obviously complicating it.

After an angry discussion the conference came to a close. I didn't know what they had decided, but they weren't planning to kill us on the spot. I had been looking for adventure, but this was more adventure than I had anticipated.

They took our food and our sleeping blankets, as well as Kanti's spear and my bow. They tied all our possessions to their lone travois, which they harnessed up to the large dog. The dog offered no objection. Apparently, the Sioux dogs often pulled travois.

If we were lucky perhaps they would steal our belongings and then leave us alone, although without our supplies we would have nothing to eat. Without our spear and bow, we couldn't even catch those funny little animals. I didn't need to worry about surviving in the wild without equipment; they were not about to abandon us. Some tribes treated foreigners like slaves. That could be worse.

The young man with the scar on his face took a long leather strap and tied my hands together. He left sufficient leather strap for a leash. Kanti was similarly tied. Scarface then said something in the Sioux language that I didn't understand, but I think it meant "follow me." He pulled on my leash in case I didn't understand.

"What do we do now, Chogan?"

"What did your dreams suggest?"

This was not a good time for sarcasm, but I was not in a good mood and I was fresh out of ideas. I was Kanti's older brother. I should be more sympathetic.

"It doesn't look like they want to hurt us, so I think we are okay for now," I said, trying to console Kanti. I wished I was as confident as I sounded.

"If we became slaves in some small village, Grandfather will never find us. We many never see Mother again."

Kanti had apparently heard the same horror stories around the campfire that I had. She was doing her best to hold back tears, but I feared they could burst forth at any moment.

"We'll do okay," I said.

We walked most of the day. Around midday we stopped near a small stream. The man with the scar on his face pointed at me and then at the small stream. I assumed he was telling me to drink the water. He released his grip on my leash, allowing me to walk down to the water. I was thirsty after the long walk. The water was cool and clean. It felt good going down my parched throat.

When I returned Scarface untied my leather bindings. He pointed to me and then to some bushes not far away. I assumed he was allowing me to attend nature's calling. He held a strong grip on Kanti's leash. Apparently, he assumed neither one of us would flee without the other.

When Kanti returned from her turn in the bushes, Scarface pointed at me and motioned for me to sit down. I don't know if I was just tired of being pointed at or thought I should try to be friendly, but I pointed toward myself and said, "Chogan." I pointed at Kanti and said, "Kanti."

Scarface thought for a moment and then repeated, "Chogan." He pointed at Kanti and said, "Kanti." He seemed satisfied with the pronunciations. My mother would be horrified if she heard me call anyone Scarface, but he offered no name for himself. I had to call him something even if it was only in my thoughts.

Kanti and I sat down as Scarface instructed, and he gave us something to eat. It was food from our canoe. Scarface and his friends helped us eat it. Kanti had extra dried meat, which she fed to the dog. The dog appeared friendly enough. It was too bad its owners did not share the dog's friendliness. After all, we were also feeding them.

"The dog reminds me of Whitefoot," Kanti said. "I think I'll name him Whitefoot." The dog was similar in appearance to a pet wolf we once had. They both had gray coats with one white paw.

"Don't get too attached to the dog. He belongs to one of these men. I'm sure he already has a name."

Our lunch break was too short. We were soon walking again toward the purple hills. Knowing our names did not lesson Scarface's anger. He frequently yanked on my leash if he thought I was walking too slowly. Along the way he had frequent arguments with the other four members of his group. I couldn't understand the words, but I assumed they were discussing our fate.

On the third day we met three more Sioux. There were further arguments. Occasionally I heard my name mentioned. They obviously had not decided what to do with us. I feared Kanti and I might suffer separate fates. They could separate us.

"Chogan, we need to do something."

Kanti was having similar thoughts. As an older brother she assumed it was my responsibility for finding a solution to our situation, but no plans came to mind. Our future didn't look promising.

"I am open to suggestions," I said.

"We need to find Takoda," Kanti said. "His grandfather is a great chieftain in the Sioux Nation. If Wambleeska were here, he would straighten everything out."

"Wambleeska?"

A tall skinny man who I called Grasshopper because of his long skinny legs must have overheard our conversation. Wambleeska apparently carried a lot of authority even in the middle of nowhere. He immediately joined the argument with Wambleeska's name frequently mentioned.

"The one word we know in the Sioux language apparently caused some commotion," I told Kanti.

"Chogan, we know two words in the Sioux language. Remember what Takoda said his name meant in his language?"

I had to think for a moment before it came to me. Takoda said is name meant *friend to everyone.*

"Wambleeska! Wambleeska takoda!" Everyone was now staring at me. The debate over our future was not over, but we were at least now part of the conversation— with a very limited vocabulary!

My hands were still bound together, but I was able to pick up a small stone. I held it up and said, "Wambleeska." Then I placed it on the ground. I pointed toward me and said, "Chogan." I pointed at Kanti and said, "Kanti." Then I placed the tips of my index and middle finger on the ground and made a walking motion toward the stone I had had labeled Wambleeska. To further emphasis my point I again pointed at Kanti and me and then pointed toward the purple hills and said Wambleeska. I didn't know if that was the direction of Wambleeska's village, but it had to be a reasonable guess. Takoda said he lived at the base of the purple hills.

After a heated discussion they apparently came to a conclusion, although the outcome was not relayed to us. It was approaching evening. Scarface unbound my hands and tossed my sleeping blanket toward me. Untying my hands provided no insight into our captors' plans for us. They had been untying us every evening. They always posted a guard at night to tend the fire and to make sure we went nowhere. They assumed running away without provisions or tools was foolhardy. I ate some dried meat and then rolled up in my sleeping blanket. It had been a strenuous day and I was tired. There was nothing more I could do or say to influence our outcome. Kanti fed some of her meat to the dog. The dog ate the meat, licked Kanti's fingers and then curled up between us. At least we had one friend in the land with no trees.

I awoke the following morning with the blunt end of a spear poking me in the ribs. I assumed Scarface wished for us to be on our way. I opened my eyes and found Kanti standing above me holding her spear. I reached to my side and found my bow and quiver resting next to my sleeping blanket.

"It appears our two-word vocabulary of the Sioux language was sufficient," Kanti said.

No comment was made by the Sioux Indians, not that we could have understood it. After we ate the breakfast offered to us, we rolled up our sleeping blankets. Scarface collected our sleeping blankets without comment and tied them to the travois. No effort was made to tie our hands. The group which I assumed had been part of a hunting or scouting party resumed their journey toward the purple hills. We were not encouraged to follow them, but neither were we discouraged. They did have our food and sleeping blankets. We decided to follow them. We were looking for Sioux Indians and they were heading in the right direction.

"What happened to the tall, skinny man?" Kanti asked.

I counted the Sioux. There were only seven. When we went to sleep there were eight Sioux. Grasshopper was missing. I didn't know if he left early this morning or late on the previous evening.

"I think he's a runner they sent ahead of us. If he's running to announce our coming to Wambleeska's village we will be fine."

"What if he's running toward some other village?" Kanti asked.

"What do your dreams tell you," I replied. I didn't wish to tell Kanti what I really thought about her question. She liked to talk about her dreams. This was a good way to change the subject.

"I'm not sure," she said. "Last night I didn't dream about rabbit holes or Takoda. I did dream about the purple hills, but the purple hills were moving. That didn't make any sense."

I momentarily stopped in my tracks. "I had a similar dream," I said. "The purple hills were waving like leaves in a summer breeze, but hills do not move."

We were having too many similar dreams to be a coincidence. We were getting closer to Takoda and his spirit was getting stronger. I wished I could understand their meaning. If his spirit was still seeking us out, Takoda had to be alive. That part of the dream was reassuring.

We continued our journey at a faster pace. Scarface now seemed in a hurry. I didn't know if that was good or bad. If Grasshopper reached a village what would he say? Finding two children who spoke a foreign language would not cause much excitement even if it were Wambleeska's village.

"Did the tall man with long legs ever mention us by name?"

"I don't think so," Kanti replied. "Why do you ask?"

"I was just wondering what he would say when he reaches his destination."

We continued walking in silence. The purple hills loomed far above us. I could now see details such a large boulders and what appeared to be trees. We couldn't get much closer. The decision on our fate couldn't be far off.

"Chogan, look at the base of the tall hill with snow on top." I looked where Kanti was pointing. "See those pointed objects? I think that's a village."

Kanti was pointing at a cluster of cone-shaped objects. They were too uniform in size and shape for natural objects. We were definitely heading for one of the Sioux villages. Perhaps there will be someone in the village who can speak our language. We had no choice but to wait and see.

We were met at the outskirts of the village by a group of children and barking dogs. They seemed to know we were coming. They were not rude, but curiosity was getting the best of them. I am sure our appearance and unusual dress warranted further exploration. We smiled at the children to signal that we were friendly even if strange.

Most of the men went their separate ways. Scarface who had shown evidence of compassion over the last two days led us to one of the cone-shaped structures. They were covered with hides that I assumed were tatanka. Scarface opened a flap to the dwelling and motioned for us to enter. He then departed; his job was done.

When our eyes adjusted to the semi-darkness we found a pleasant appearing woman about Mother's age. She was alone and spoke nothing. I assumed she did not speak our language and knew any attempt at conversation would be fruitless.

"We need to do something." Kanti could never tolerate silence.

"If you think you can speak the Sioux language, this is not the time to hold back." This was also not the time for sarcasm, but I had nothing else to offer.

"Kanti," Kanti said as she pointed to herself. She pointed at me. "Chogan."

The woman pointed toward herself and said, "Chumani." I nodded. Then she pointed to a bedroll along the side of the lodge and repeated her name. I looked around and discovered three more bedrolls. She went around the lodge naming the bedrolls. She caught our attention when she mentioned Takoda and Wambleeska.

"Kanti, I think we have found Takoda's lodge. Chumani must be his mother."

Chumani behaved like a typical mother. We were her guests and would be treated accordingly. She brought out more dried meat than even Kanti could eat. I could now recognize the taste of dried tatanka. She provided water from a container that I assumed was a tatanka stomach. It was not cool, but I was thirsty. It seemed that everything came from the tatanka: food, clothing, shelter, and containers.

"What do we do now?" Kanti asked. "Where's Takoda?" Patience was not one of Kanti's virtues.

"Perhaps he is hunting or checking snares like we do. We don't sit in our wigwam all day."

I looked around Takoda's lodge. It was simple like a wigwam, but there were no sleeping benches. People slept on the ground. That would be too cold where we lived. A small cooking fire burned tatanka chips. The smoke from the fire circled around and eventually exited the lodge through a hole at the top of the cone.

Chumani took my sleeping blanket and placed it near the side of the lodge. She did likewise with Kanti's sleeping blanket. Then she again named all the bedrolls, ending with ours. Apparently, we would be sleeping here tonight. Mothers behaved the same in all cultures. This was her home. She was in charge and we were welcome guests. I sat down next to my bedroll and waited. Kanti did likewise.

It was an awkward situation, since we had no way of communicating. We did not have to wait long. Soon the flap to the lodge opened and Takoda stepped inside. His grandfather followed closely behind him.

"Chogan, Kanti, this is such a surprise. I ran to the village as soon as I heard, although I feared it could not be true at first," Takoda said. "You have come a long distance. Did you come alone?

Takoda was full of questions. It would require most of the evening to answer all of them. We were just happy to see him alive. He seemed to be in good health and not in any immediate danger. We sat around the small fire and told of our dreams. Takoda's grandfather lit his pipe and listened. When we finished everyone sat in silence as they pondered what we had said. Finally Takoda's grandfather broke the silence.

"You have traveled a great distance," he said. "Has your grandfather come with you?"

"Grandfather is following us," I replied. Maybe if I voiced it out loud it would become true. "We left in a hurry." I didn't mention that Kanti left without approval.

"Your grandfather is like a brother to me. It will be good to see him again When he arrives we will have a feast in his honor and celebrate old times. In the morning I will send runners to all the villages to ensure his safe passage." Wambleeska inhaled deeply on his pipe and closed his eyes in thought. He reminded me of Grandfather. He would share his wisdom and thoughts, but there would be no rushing him.

"Many times dreams have no meaning," he said, "but I am troubled by the persistence of your dreams. Takoda sits before us in good health, and rabbit holes should provide no danger to a boy who is almost a man."

Wambleeska inhaled on his pipe and closed his eyes again. I assumed there was more wisdom to come. He exhaled slowly and opened his eyes.

"The rabbit has many predators. It must always be wary, but its life is not dictated by fear. The rabbit must live its life to the fullest or its life has no value. Takoda, your friends' dreams makes me worry. Your life may indeed be in danger, but like the rabbit you must live out your life. And like the rabbit you must be wary until this danger has passed."

"Grandfather, how am I to know when the danger has passed?" Takoda asked.

"Your spirit has reached out to your friends. The same spirit will tell them when the danger has passed."

I wasn't sure I liked being entrusted with Takoda's fate. Most of my dreams were meaningless. Purple hills waving like leaves in a gentle breeze did not impart much valuable information.

"Chogan, this morning Grandfather and I were scouting for tatanka," Takoda said. "That is why I wasn't here to greet you and Kanti, but if I had known you were coming I would have let Grandfather scout them on his own. Tomorrow there will be a great hunt. We will kill many tatanka and provide enough meat to feed the entire village. I would be honored to have you join our hunt."

"I am coming too," Kanti said. It was not a request; it was a statement. She was never one to be left out. Sometimes I find this embarrassing.

"Kanti, you will be welcome on the hunt. Many women participate."

That prompted Kanti to describe her role in our tatanka hunt lest Takoda think girls couldn't provide a significant role in the hunt. Sometimes I wish Kanti were more modest, although she did play a dangerous and vital role in that hunt. We talked to Takoda until late in the evening.

Chapter Nine

I awoke to activity all around me. Kanti was up as I would have expected. I looked around; no one else was sleeping. Everyone was preparing for the big hunt. Kanti bonded with Takoda's mother despite the language barrier. She was talking non-stop in Ojibway and Takoda's mother was replying in Sioux. Neither one could understand the other, but hand and finger gestures bridged the gap. They were preparing meals for the wigwam residents, and that included me.

"Chumani made breakfast."

I assumed Chumani was Takoda's mother. She introduced herself the previous day, but I had forgotten. Kanti was better at remembering names. Kanti gave me a bowl of strange food. There were roots and vegetables I had never eaten before. I assumed the pieces of meat were tatanka. The survival of the Sioux Nation depended on those shaggy deer. Takoda was busy talking to his father and grandfather, so I ate my food in silence. They were obviously discussing the coming hunt. When I finished eating I returned the bowl to Chumani. I smiled and made a gesture I hoped would be interpreted as a thank you.

I followed Takoda and his father as they exited the wigwam. Most of the village was gathering for the hunt. Hunting should be work, but I saw much excitement. There were men, women and many dogs. It didn't take Kanti long to find Whitefoot. Kanti bribed him with dried meat from her shoulder bag. Takoda's mother had provided Kanti with an endless supply. She probably assumed she could replenish her supply after the hunt.

According to Takoda, Whitefoot belonged to Scarface. Scarface was a likeable person once I got to know him. I now felt guilty about calling him Scarface, but I still didn't know his real name.

"Is your grandfather coming with us?" He had remained in the wigwam. I found that strange, since he planned the hunt.

"He led the scouting party that found the tatanka," Takoda replied. "His knees are getting old and he cannot take frequent long walks. He's leaving the tatanka hunting to younger men."

"Where are the tatanka?" I asked. I looked in all directions, but saw no tatanka. There were many small hills surrounding the village. The small hills were insignificant compared to the beautiful purple hills that reached up to kiss the sky, but the small hills could easily hide a herd of tatanka.

"Yesterday we found a small herd not far from here. It's a short walk," Takoda said. "If all goes as planned, we will isolate nine or ten tatanka from the main group. Then we will use all our people and dogs to herd them to a bluff overlooking a small creek. If we can force them to stampede toward the bluff, they will fall to their deaths. It is safer than trying to spear them. Tatanka can be dangerous, so don't get close to them." My thoughts returned to Kanti teasing a bull no more than ten paces in front of her. What if she had slipped or missed her grip on the rock. It seemed even more foolish in hindsight, but we were hungry.

We followed the crowd toward the northeast. The outing appeared more like a party than a hunt. Men and women gathered into small groups. I couldn't understand what they were saying, but there was much laughter. Laughter is the same in any language. Kanti and I followed Takoda, and Whitefoot followed Kanti's pouch of dried tatanka. Scarface didn't seem to mind. Most of the other dogs gathered in small packs much like their human masters. It had the makings of an adventurous day.

The sun had risen high in the sky, and I had yet to see any tatanka. I was beginning to wonder if we had missed them. I could find my way in the deep woods, but here every hill looked the same. The village had disappeared behind us. I wouldn't be able to find it without help. None of the men or women around me looked concerned.

"We've walked most of the morning, and I haven't seen any tatanka," I said. "Have we missed them?"

"Your eyes don't know what to look for," Takoda said. "The tatanka are grazing in the distance. See those brown spots at the base of that hill?"

Takoda pointed to a shallow valley not far from where we were standing. As I looked closely, I could see some of the brown spots I had assumed were rocks were slowly moving. Others had also seen the tatanka. The chatter among the women had increased. The men whispered to each other. That seemed silly, since the tatanka couldn't hear them at that distance.

"What do we do now?" I asked. I was becoming excited. We wouldn't be hunting one tatanka but many of them. I was sure this adventure would be worth telling around many campfires when I returned home.

"The men in the front will give directions," Takoda replied. "We have some men who have been following the herd since yesterday. They separated nine or ten tatanka from the main herd. When we catch up to them, we'll encourage the tatanka to walk toward the bluff." Takoda pointed to a grassy knoll where the ground appeared to drop off. "The tatanka are dangerous animals, but they'll be intimidated by so many people. If all goes as planned, the tatanka will walk away from us and toward the bluff. When they get real close, we'll yell and scream. The tatanka should panic and run toward the bluff. The animals in front will see the drop off and stop, but the tatanka behind them will push them over the cliff."

Nine or ten tatanka would provide plenty of meat, but this was for a village twice the size of my village. Kanti with her boundless energy worked her way in front of the villagers, with Whitefoot clinging to her side. Every hundred paces Kanti bribed him with a piece of dried meat from her shoulder pouch. Takoda and I followed twenty paces behind her. I don't know how we got so far in front of the main group. Given a choice, I would have preferred following the group instead of taking the lead. I assumed Takoda knew what he was doing.

Kanti and Whitefoot descended into a small ravine in front of us, disappearing from sight. I didn't think much of it until I heard Whitefoot barking aggressively.

Something had gotten his attention. Takoda and I ran toward the sound, although I failed to appreciate the urgency. When we arrived at the top of the ravine I found Kanti lying on the ground with her spear in hand. She must have tripped on one of the many holes dug by those strange creatures. A large bull stood in front of her, and he did not look pleased.

"Quick, Chogan, we need to get Kanti out of there." Takoda ran toward Kanti while yelling something in his Sioux language. I ran after Takoda. Out of the corner of my eye I saw men running in our direction, but they would not arrive in time. Takoda and I reached Kanti at the same time. We each grabbed a shoulder and lifted her to her feet while Kanti waved her spear menacingly at the angry animal. Kanti is brave, but lacks wisdom. There was no way she would stop a raging bull with her small spear.

We pulled Kanti backward while facing the bull. Grandfather said I should back away from a bear and not run. Bears interpret running as a sign of weakness and will give chase. I hoped that wisdom applied to tatanka.

"Can you walk?" I asked.

"I twisted my ankle."

I assumed that meant no. The tatanka was standing ten paces from us and pawing the ground. His head was lowered and he was snorting vigorously. I didn't have to be an expert in tatanka mannerisms to recognize the bull's aggressive behavior.

"Takoda, take Kanti. I'll see if I can distract the bull." I had no plan on how to distract the bull, but even if I did, it would have been too late. The tatanka bull gave out one last snort and charged toward us. At such a short distance there was little time to react. My first thought was to get low to the ground. I feared the bull's hooves less than I did its horns. I could feel the bull's hot breath on my face. I braced myself for the impact with the huge animal, but at the last second it turned to my right. Whitefoot was nipping at its front leg. It was something our pet wolf would have done.

I felt strong hands pull me backward. The men with spears had arrived. The tatanka, realizing it was vastly outnumbered, trotted off to join the rest of the herd. I looked toward Kanti and Takoda; they were both safe. Kanti was rewarding Whitefoot with several large strips of dried tatanka. I found the choice of dried meat appropriate.

"Chogan, you are bleeding!"

I didn't know what Kanti was talking about until I felt the steady drip of fluid from my forehead. I reached up to wipe it away and then looked at my hand. It was red.

"The tatanka's horn must have scraped your forehead just before it turned." Takoda made a pad of dry grass and handed it to me. "Press this against the wound. When it stops bleeding Mother can sew your skin together. She is good at that."

I thanked Takoda and pressed the patch against my wound. There was little pain, so I assumed the wound was superficial. I had been lucky. If it hadn't been for Whitefoot, I could have been killed. I gave him a pat on the head. He seemed to understand, although he preferred the thank-you Kanti produced from her pouch.

The villagers had thirty tatanka separated from the herd and were gradually urging them toward the cliff. Thirty seemed like a lot of tatanka. When the animals were twenty paces from the edge, one of the men yelled something in the Sioux language. Everyone began to scream and wave their hands. The animals panicked and broke into a run. When the first animals reached the rim, they tried to stop, but they were pushed over the edge by the tatanka behind them, just as Takoda had predicted. I didn't see them hit the bottom of the ravine, but there was ample noise and dust. The villagers whooped and yelled as they converged on the injured animals.

When I arrived at the rim's edge, men were piercing the surviving tatanka with spears or cutting their throats with knives. Women were already skinning some of the dead animals. There would be plenty of meat and skins for the village. Takoda had deserted us. Apparently he had another errand to do. Kanti and I stood alone at the top of the bluff watching the scene below in wonder. It was an efficient way of hunting—maybe too efficient.

"Do you think they can carry all that meat back to the village?" Kanti asked.

Tatanka were huge animals—and there were thirty of them in the ravine below us. Spread out over time the meat could be dried and preserved, but I couldn't envision the limited number of people in the village processing that much meat before it spoiled or was claimed by wolves and coyotes. Grandfather always said we should kill no more than we could eat. He wouldn't be happy with what we were witnessing.

"They have a different lifestyle," I replied to Kanti's question. "It is not for us to judge."

"My mother will fix your wound," Takoda said.

We were watching the slaughter below and hadn't seen Takoda approach. His mother and two other women were with him. Chumani gently removed the pad I had been holding against my cut. Most of the bleeding had stopped. She motioned for me to sit down on a large rock and then she began to fuss with my wound. Her facial expressions and concern reminded me of my own mother. I guess mothers are the same in any tribe. She talked not-stop in her native Sioux language. Two of the attending women disappeared. Apparently, Chumani sent them on a mission in my behalf. I assumed Takoda would translate if Chumani had instructions for me. Takoda noticed my concern.

"Mother sent one woman to fetch water from the river to wash your wound," Takoda said. "The other woman is fetching hair from the tail of a tatanka to sew your skin together."

"I hope it is not from the bull that gashed me. I don't think he liked me." My attempt at humor fell flat although only Kanti and Takoda understood what I said.

One of the women returned with a bowl of water and fluff from a cattail. Chumani moistened the cattail fluff and dabbed at my wound. I would be lying if I said it didn't hurt. When she was satisfied the wound was properly cleaned, she took a sliver of bone and pierced my skin. I couldn't see what she was doing, but I had watched mother stitch more than one wound. She used chin hair from a moose. I don't know if that worked better than tail hair from a tatanka. I waited patiently until Chumani put down her bone needle. I assumed she was done. I nodded and bowed gently.

"Takoda, can you please thank your mother for me." Takoda conversed briefly with his mother in their native language.

"Mother says it was an honor to be of assistance to our guest, but she is afraid it will leave a scar."

I wasn't worried about the scar. It would be visual proof of my adventure with an angry tatanka. I walked down to the stream hoping there would be a quiet pool where I could admire my badge of honor, but the river was too swift to provide a good reflection. I finally gave up on my endeavor. Grandfather would have called it vanity, but I was proud of my first conflict with a tatanka.

I looked around for Kanti and Takoda. They were assisting Takoda's father who was skinning one of the larger animals. I walked over to assist. I grabbed a corner of the hide and helped pulled it from the carcass. Deer and rabbits look much smaller once skinned, but the tatanka was still a large animal. It would provide plenty of meat, and we had run thirty of them off the cliff.

"Takoda, there are many animals. Can your village use all of them?" I asked.

"We can use over half of them," he replied. "The wolves and coyotes will eat much of what is left."

Even a large wolf pack couldn't eat fifteen leftover tatanka. I was almost killed by an angry tatanka, but I felt no grudge. They were noble animals trying to survive. They should not be needlessly wasted. Takoda must have seen the concern on my face.

"There are many tatanka," he said. "No matter how many we kill, there will always be tatanka."

I hoped he was right. We finished skinning the tatanka in silence. We cut off the large segments of meat and tied them to travois. Now I knew why there were so many dogs. They dragged over half of the travois. The other half was human power. Kanti and I each carried our share of the meat.

"The women will slice and dry the meat after we return to the village," Takoda said. "We will celebrate and have a great feast tonight."

Chapter Ten

The travois I dragged back to the village had less meat than most travois, but I was still relieved when we reached Takoda's teepee. It had not been one of my better days. An angry tatanka almost killed me. I would wear a scar on my forehead as a constant reminder of that encounter. That was too much excitement even for me. I opened the leather flap covering the door of the teepee and stepped inside. It took a moment or two for my eyes to adjust to the dim light. Even then I was hard to believe what I was seeing. Grandfather and Wambleeska were sitting around a small fire smoking pipes and chatting, sometimes in our language and sometimes in the Sioux language. My cousin, Hassun, was sitting beside them.

"Grandfather, you found us!"

"You marked a good trail," Grandfather replied. "We followed you until you left your canoe at the river bank, but my good friend Wambleeska sent runners to all the villages. Many people were searching for us. We followed smoke to a Sioux village, and then one of the younger men guided us to a warm welcome in this teepee."

I felt like all was well with the world now that Grandfather and Hassun had arrived. Making such important decisions as I had been forced to make were stressful. Now Grandfather would be making those decisions. I could resume being a boy of twelve winters.

"Are you angry with me, Grandfather?" Kanti asked. She had been standing quietly by the doorway, unsure if she should enter. It was obvious she knew the answer to her question. She was consumed with guilt. She looked close to tears.

"I was," Grandfather said, "until my good friend Wambleeska reminded me of a boy not much older than Chogan who left his village and traveled to this land with no trees. I did not travel with the blessing of my family either. I made my trip without the aid of Winnebago merchants. That was far more dangerous than what you did." That seemed to assure Kanti she was welcome in the teepee. She stepped inside and cautiously sat beside me and Takoda.

"Grandfather, my dreams are so real. I had to do something to help Takoda."

"Kanti, your heart was pure, but sometimes you act as impulsively as a young river otter."

"Yes, Grandfather."

"You will grow in wisdom as you grow older, but what is done is done. Once water flows over a waterfall it can never return," Grandfather said. "Tell me about your dreams. Wambleeska has told me much, but I would like to hear from you."

Kanti told of her dreams from the beginning. She felt inspired now that people were taking her dreams seriously. I added what knowledge I had and told of my dreams, although they were not as vivid as Kanti's dreams. When we finished Grandfather and Wambleeska quietly smoked their pipes. Neither one was in a hurry to offer an impulsive opinion.

"Many dreams have no significance," Grandfather said, breaking the silence. "They are little more than tricks our minds play upon us as we sleep. But dreams with such persistence are not usual. The spirit world is obviously trying to communicate with you. You and Chogan once saved Takoda's life. That creates a great bond with your spirits. Takoda is or soon will be in grave danger." Wambleeska nodded in agreement.

"Today we were almost gored by a bull tatanka," Takoda said. "Perhaps that was the danger."

"But you were only in danger because we ran to rescue Kanti," I said. "The spirit world did not send us here to place you in danger."

"There was no rabbit hole," Kanti added. "There must be a rabbit hole. The rabbit hole was in every dream."

"What about the purple hills waving like leaves in a summer breeze?" I asked. "I have seen that in four or five dreams."

There was much discussion. Everyone had an opinion, but we agreed nothing in the dreams made sense. If the spirit world was speaking to us, it was speaking to us in a foreign language. Wambleeska was conspicuous in his silence. He was chief of the mighty Sioux Nation and the grandfather of our good friend, Takoda. It was difficult to believe he did not have an opinion. Finally he raised his hand and everyone in the teepee ceased talking.

"Chogan and Kanti have traveled a great distance. They have endured many hardships to warn their friend of grave danger. With their actions they have placed great honor upon themselves. We are thankful. Chogan and Kanti as well as their grandfather will always be welcome in our teepee."

Kanti had been consumed with guilt. Now she was sitting taller. When I think back on our long journey, it seemed we had accomplished the impossible. I had feared our return trip without the aid of the Winnebago merchants, but now we had Grandfather and Hassun to help us find our way home.

"Much of what Chogan and Kanti tell us from their dreams does not make sense," Wambleeska continued. "It does tell us Takoda is in great danger. The dreams are too ambiguous to identify the danger. Takoda must remain constantly vigilant. My brother's grandchildren are wise for their years. My grandson and his family are honored by their friendship. You will be our honored guests for as long as you wish to stay. "

"As usual, my brother speaks with great wisdom," Grandfather said.

"I promise to stay out of rabbit holes," Takoda offered.

I wished he would take our warning more seriously, although our warning was vague and offered no altered course of action to prevent injury or death. If he had experienced Kanti's dreams or even mine, he might change his attitude.

"Grandfather, how long can we stay here? Can we see the boiling mud and the spouting water?"

Grandfather had visited the land with no trees and the purple hills in his youth. He told many tales of his adventures around the campfires. My favorite tale was of mud so hot it boiled and spouts of water and steam shooting high into the sky. I have a good imagination, but I still have difficulty visualizing such places. If it were anyone other than Grandfather I would not have believed him.

"It is only a four-day walk from here," Takoda said. "Grandfather, can we take them to the sacred place with the yellow stone and boiling water?"

Being the older brother, I was in charge during the trip to the land with no trees. Now Grandfather was here. It would be his decision. I could only ask. I knew better than to nag.

"We have come a long way," Grandfather said. "Chogan and Kanti will return to the land of trees and lakes with many memories. It would be a shame if the sacred place with the yellow stone and boiling water was not one of them."

"It is settled then," Wambleeska said. "We will leave when the sun rises in the morning. It has been a long time since I have been to that sacred place. The strange behavior of the land never ceases to amaze visitors."

Takoda said he had been their twice, but he was just as excited as Kanti and I were. We should have gone to bed early to prepare for the long journey. Instead we talked long into the night. Totally exhausted, we eventually fell asleep.

Morning came early. As usual, Kanti was up before rest of us. She was helping Chumani prepare breakfast. It was a big meal with fresh chunks of tatanka and steamed roots I could not identify. We would need the big meal to sustain us on the pending trip. According to Takoda the trail was too rugged for a person or dog to pull a travois.

We would have to carry all food and bed rolls on our backs. Kanti and I still had our moose blankets that we used for sleeping. Kanti filled both of our pouches with dried tatanka. Chumani and some of the other women in the village had prepared fresh pemmican. They must have made it during the night from the freshly-killed tatanka.

There were seven of us in the party. Hassun and Scarface would be our scouts. They would find the best trails and mountain passes. Takoda said it would be a difficult four days with many canyons and rivers to cross. What he was describing as difficult, I was looking forward to with excitement. We would be climbing those purple hills that reached up to kiss the sky. It was still summer, but we might see snow on the tops. I discovered Scarface was Takoda's cousin. I was really beginning to like him. He had seen twenty-two winters and was similar to Hassun in age. Despite the language barrier, they were becoming good friends. If there is sufficient desire, thoughts can be conveyed without language.

We began our journey by walking west toward the purple hills. Up close they are no different than any other land; except these hills were covered with large outcrops of granite and our trail twisted uphill seemingly forever. In the land of lakes and trees we have hills, but it takes little effort to reach the top and then it was all downhill. These hills did not have a top. We climbed most of the day, and we still had not reached the top. When I looked back, it appeared like I could see forever. I wondered if my home of lakes and trees was visible in the distance.

We reached our campsite by nightfall. I was exhausted, but my excitement wouldn't allow me to rest.

There was too much to see and explore. Scarface and Hassun had hiked ahead and picked this grassy area for its flat surface. Most other area would have us rolling down the hill in our sleep. But this campsite was perfect and came with a magnificent view. Wambleeska spoke briefly to his grandson in their native tongue.

"My grandfather wants us to find some firewood," Takoda said.

"We should stay together," I replied. "Lead the way. Kanti and I will help carry the wood back to our camp."

We had seen many trees as we climbed the purple hill, but now they were few and far between. Takoda led us to a ravine that offered some stunted trees, many of which were dead. We broke off the dead limbs.

"Why are there so few trees here? They were all over as we climbed the hill," I asked.

"I don't know," Takoda replied. "If we climb any higher, they will all be gone. Without wood or tatanka chips there will be no more fire until we walk down on the other side."

There was so much about this land that fascinated me. By Takoda's village there was only grass. As we climbed the purple hills we found trees, but the trees were short and thin in diameter, nothing like the big oaks and maples back home. Now we were switching back to all grass. Even more intriguing, I could see patches of snow in the near distance. Takoda said we would reach them tomorrow. I was looking forward to that.

After we each had a small armful of firewood, we headed back to camp. There was not enough wood to keep a fire going throughout the night, but the fire should take the chill out of the ground we would sleep on. Hassun quickly started a fire at the base of a small granite outcrop that rose vertically from the grass. It was short enough that a tall man could see over the top of the granite, but the vertical sides reflected the heat from our fire. If we bedded down between the wall and the fire we would remain warm. Wambleeska said it would get cold and we would need the fire.

Everyone opened their backpacks and snacked on the pemmican. There was little talk. It had been a long uphill climb and we were exhausted. I was surprised how well Wambleeska and Grandfather managed. They were not as young as the rest of us. Takoda predicted we would reach the top of the purple hill no later than noon tomorrow after which the trail would be much easier. I hoped he was right. He was also predicting we would be walking in snow. I had seen lots of snow, but only in the winter time.

After we had eaten our fill we quenched our thirst from a small stream. The water was cold and clear. It tasted good. Takoda said the water came from the melted snow above us. If he had never been to see the boiling mud before, I would have questioned his authority, but he had been right so far.

Kanti and I unrolled our sleeping blankets next to each other, although Whitefoot claimed a small swatch of grass between us. I was sure he chose the spot more because of Kanti than me—she was the one who kept bribing him with dried meat from her unending supply. If the night got cold, a warm dog is always an asset. He reminded me so much of the pet wolf we once had. Takoda unrolled his bed roll on the other side of me. Sleeping shoulder to shoulder conserves body heat Grandfather told me when I was very young. Experience confirmed his wisdom many times over.

The sun sets in the west behind the purple hills, so night came quickly. In the land of lakes and trees it can be difficult to see much of the night sky unless canoeing on a lake after dark. There was no moon tonight to subdue the fainter stars, and the air was pure and clear. I had never seen so many stars as what had come forth to rule the night.

"There's a shooting star," Takoda said.

I had just seen it out of the corner of my eye. I was just about to reply to Takoda's comment when another large meteor burned a path across the sky. I think everyone saw that one as there were grunts of satisfaction and approval by all except Whitefoot. He was already asleep.

"This is the time of the summer when we will see many streaks of light across the sky," Wambleeska said.

Takoda's grandfather was right as we saw one after the other. Some traced across most of the sky and left trails of smoke. I was afraid to close my eyes for fear that I would miss some of the heavenly show.

"Our people believe shooting stars are gifts sent to someone on Earth by the Great Spirit," I told Takoda.

"That is a lot of gifts," Kanti said. "I wonder if any of them are for me."

"I have already received my gift," Takoda said. "I wanted to see the boiling mud and the water that spouts high in the air once more. I can't think of two people I would rather share that experience with than you and Chogan."

We lay on the grass each with our own thoughts and watched the multitude of shooting stars streak across the sky until sleep overtook us.

Chapter Eleven

When I awoke the sky was clear, but my bedroll was covered with dew. Without clouds, it wouldn't take long for the morning sun to dry the moose skin. Takoda was awake but unwilling to abandon the warmth of his tatanka-skin blanket. I wondered if tatanka skin was warmer than moose skin. I would have to get a tatanka blanket before I left. I would be the only one in our village with such a blanket.

Trees didn't grow on the tops of the purple hills, and without tatanka chips, there would be no more fires until we walked down the other side of the purple hill. Everyone else was up and scurrying about. Kanti had given Whitefoot his breakfast; he was now off exploring his surroundings. Even dogs found our trip enjoyable.

"Kanti, where are Hassun and Scarface?" I was glad Scarface didn't understand our language. I didn't want to insult him, but I still didn't know his real name.

"You mean Hassun and Paytah? Paytah means fire in the Sioux language."

It shouldn't surprise me that Kanti knew his name. She was learning many Sioux words. If we spent much time in the land with no trees, Kanti would be fluent in the language before we left.

"Yeah, where are Hassun and Paytah?"

"They left at first light to scout the trail. They'll leave markers for us to follow."

Everyone appeared eager to reach the top of the purple hill, so I quickly ate my pemmican and strapped my bedroll to my backpack. Grandfather and Wambleeska were conversing with half of their sentences in our language and half in the Sioux Language. I envied anyone who could speak more than one tongue.

As soon as Takoda strapped on his backpack, we began our way up the trail following the markers left by Hassun and Paytah. Takoda said we would reach the top before noon, but I could only see more uphill. The purple hills truly did reach up to kiss the sky. The tops of many of the hills were covered in white.

"We will soon be into the snow,' Takoda promised.

I nodded as if this was not an unusual event. I found it difficult to believe snow could exist in the summer. The sun was warm, and we weren't dressed for winter, yet in front of us were large fields of snow. Takoda lived in a strange land.

The trail markers left by Hassun and Paytah pointed toward a shallow ravine with granite outcrops on both sides. The section between the outcrops was as white as a swan swimming in the afternoon sun. We would soon be walking across snow with little more than our summer clothing. If I told this around a campfire back home, no one would believe me.

I wondered if the snow would be too deep. In our land of lakes and trees we needed snowshoes in deep snow, but when I stepped on the snow I found a thick crust. The snow had been melting during the day and refreezing at night. I was about to take a second step when something hit me in the back of the head. I looked up just in time to see a snowball hit Takoda in the shoulder.

We were caught in a crossfire. Hassun was pelting snowballs from the granite ledge on the right and Paytah was throwing snowballs from the other side. We had little choice but to return fire. The snow beneath the crust was perfect for making snowballs. Hassun and Paytah had the advantage of the high ground, but we soon discovered they had limited snowballs and our supple was endless. They eventually surrendered to our superior force. Grandfather and Wambleeska, maintaining that no one wins in wars, wisely observed the battle from the sidelines. After his supply of snowballs was exhausted, Paytah climbed down from his lofty perch to confer with Grandfather and Wambleeska.

"My cousin is saying we have reached the top of the purple hill. We will soon begin our journey down the other side," Takoda said.

Takoda's words created much excitement. We still had several days before we reached the land of boiling mud and spouting water, but the uphill climb had taken a toll on all of us. I was amazed how well Grandfather and Wambleeska had fared. Their joints and muscles were not as young as ours.

The snow didn't last long, and my fear of deep snow proved unfounded. The crust was so thick that even large individuals such as Grandfather and Wambleeska easily walked across the top. Wambleeska said we were fortunate not to have encountered a snowstorm. Such storms can make the passes over the tops of the purple hills impassable. Major snowstorms in the summer were difficult to believe, but we were walking on snow. That should also be impossible. There was so much that was new and unimaginable in this land with no trees.

Walking down a hill is easier that walking up a hill, but if the slope is very steep much of the advantage is lost. A new set of muscles is needed to keep from falling forward. Both Grandfather and Wambleeska had acquired walking sticks before ascending the purple hill. I considered a walking stick one more object to carry. Now I could see their age had provided them with more wisdom than I had accumulated in my limited experience. We will retrace our steps on the way home. Then I will also be wiser.

Hassun and Paytah ran ahead to find a campsite for the evening. They were young and had long legs, which allowed them to run and walk faster than Grandfather or Wambleeska. They quickly disappeared in the distance. I was hoping our evening campsite would have access to wood or tatanka chips. The heavy dew and cold temperature from the previous night had made sleeping difficult. I was looking forward to a campfire with real heat. Pemmican also tasted better if heated until the fat began to melt. I preferred hot meals.

The trees returned in the same manner as they disappeared. First as small shrubs and stunted trees followed by taller trees. I missed the tall oaks and maples in the land of trees and lakes. They were nonexistent here. I noticed many dead and broken trees. We should have plenty of wood for a fire.

Toward the end of the day our trail led us into a large valley. There were many aspen trees, but there were also large grassy areas. I saw several tatanka, but no large herds. What caught my attention were the strange animals with prong horns. I had not seen them before. They looked more like deer than the tatanka did.

"What are those animals?" I pointed to one of the closer animals.

"Those are antelope," Takoda replied. "They are very tasty. They are also very fast and difficult to kill with an arrow or spear."

I envisioned an antelope roasting over an open fire, but Takoda was right, they were too far away to hit with an arrow and in the open grassland there was no way to sneak up on them. I would have to be happy with warm pemmican.

It was difficult following Hassun and Paytah's trail in the deep grass. Any stone or stick pointers would be well hidden. Fortunately they kept the trail close to trees or wooded areas where they could blaze a mark on the bark. The land along the valley floor was flat and smooth and we made good time. The sun was beginning to set when we saw smoke in the distance.

"Hassun and Paytah have a campfire waiting for us," Wambleeska said. "We will no longer have to look for marks on the trees."

I hoped he was right. If that was their fire we did not have far to go. I was enjoying the adventure, but my feet could take only so much excitement. I wondered if anyone else had tired feet. I didn't want to be the first one to complain; a boy has his pride.

It was just getting dark when we arrived at the campsite. Hassun and Paytah were grinning and sitting around their campfire. I expected to be impressed with the fire, but even more impressive was the fresh meat roasting over the fire.

"Where did you guys get the meat!"

Paytah couldn't understand what I was saying, but the look on my face didn't require an interpreter.

"I lay on the ground covered with my moose skin bedroll while my good friend circled behind the antelope and gently herded it in my direction, Hassun said. "They are no more difficult to bring down than our deer as long as you can get close. It ran fewer than fifty paces with my arrow in its chest before it fell to the ground."

Only the two hind legs were roasting over the fire. Grease was dripping down and spattering in the fire. Hassun and Paytah had been here for some time as the meat appeared fully roasted. They had thrown the remains of the carcass to the side, which gave me an opportunity to see this strange animal up close. I poked at the head with a stick. It looked similar to our deer. They were slender and had long skinny legs built for running. Unlike our deer they didn't have antlers that divided into many twigs. Instead their antlers rose up as a single prong with a single divide at the top. Takoda said they keep their antlers all year and don't shed them like our deer, and both males and females have the horns.

Other than Whitefoot no one else showed interest in the carcass. They were more interested in eating the antelope. I had to admit, the roasting meat smelled good. Paytah handed me a short stick and then cut off a piece with his obsidian knife. The meat was too hot to hold in my hands, so I quickly stabbed it with my stick. It tasted like venison. We ate until we could eat no more. Kanti gave some of the cooked meat to Whitefoot, although I think he would have been content eating the raw meat from the carcass.

Takoda, Kanti, and I gathered more firewood. Takoda predicted it would not get as cold now than we had walked down from the hilltop. I still liked a campfire and if there was wood left over in the morning, we could have another warm meal. The land of boiling mud and spouting water was a long way off, but it felt closer now that we had climbed over the purple hills.

On the fourth day we saw a giant bear in the distance. It was larger than the bears from the land of lakes and trees. I had once encountered one of these bears in the land of lakes and trees. It had somehow wandered the vast distance to arrive at our land. I confronted it along a trail. I didn't want to repeat that experience. They frighten me.

"We'll walk around the bear," Wambleeska said. "It'll leave us alone if we leave it alone."

I wished I shared his confidence. At least the bear was a fair distance away. We gave it a wide berth as we walked around it. I continued watching the bear out of the corner of my eye, but it only scratched at the ground, totally ignoring us. I felt safer once we had increased our distance, but if there was one bear, there were probably more. Logic told me a smart bear would not attack six armed individuals—seven if you count Kanti and her spear. The land was mostly tall grass with small patches of trees. As long as we stayed in the grass we would not surprise any bear and no bear would surprise us.

We continued on. Hassun and Paytah were scouting ahead of us as usual. We would reunite when the sun was high in the sky. Paytah had visited the sacred land many times. I trusted he would keep us from getting lost. It was a big country, and so much of it looked the same. I would easily get lost.

"There is smoke up ahead," Takoda said. "Hassun and Paytah must have started another campfire."

This observation created much talk and speculation, but Wambleeska just smiled and keep on walking. I had discovered he was much like Grandfather; he was full of knowledge that he infrequently shared. When he did speak, wise people listened. I assumed he had knowledge that he was not willing to share at the moment. We continued walking toward the smoke.

"There are two fires," Kanti said.

The white smoke rose up and twisted with the air currents. If I looked closely it did appear to be two separate fires. That made little sense and it was a waste of firewood. I had to admit it did pique my curiosity.

"I can see three fires—no, four," Takoda pointed to the various white strands rising up from the grassy meadow. The closer we came, the more white columns we saw. Hassun and Paytah would surely have an explanation for us. I could see them in the distance walking toward us.

"You need to be careful where you walk," Hassun said once he got close, "and watch the dog. The ground is very hot in some places. It may burn the dog's paws."

"Why did you start so many fires?" I asked.

"We didn't," Hassun replied. "That's steam, not smoke. The steam is coming from holes in the ground."

We must have reached the land of the boiling mud and spouting water. I could see no mud, and the steam was impressive, but I expected real water not steam. I felt the ground; it was warm, just as Hassun said. It wasn't hot enough to burn Whitefoot's paws, but we were only approaching the steam vents. The ground could get hotter as we got closer.

Kanti made a collar from her scarf and then tied that to a short piece of twine. I thought Whitefoot would resent the leash, but as long as Kanti bribed him with dried meat, he was happy. Kanti took off her moccasins. I looked at her questioningly.

"If it gets too hot for my feet, it'll be too hot for Whitefoot," she replied when she saw my inquisitive look.

Paytah and Hassun led us through the field of steam vents. We were able to breathe some of the steam as we got closer. It was not a pleasant experience. It reminded me of spoiled duck eggs. We passed several crystal-clear pools of water. It would have looked like good drinking water if not for the bubbles of gas rising from the depths. The edges of the pools were coated with a yellow substance. I felt the ground beneath my moccasins; it was hot.

"We need to keep Whitefoot back," I said. Kanti was holding him ten paces from the pool. Her feet must have gotten hot. I wasn't sure I wanted to get any closer. If I were to fall into the pool it would have cooked me before anyone could fish me out. Despite the potential danger, the field of steam vents and hot bubbling pools were mesmerizing. How could I describe this to my friends when I returned home? No one would believe me.

"We need to move on," Wambleeska said. "We must find a camp for tonight. There will be more to see tomorrow."

"Paytah and I found a spot not far from here where trees will shade us from dew," Hassun said.

Paytah and Hassun led us around the steam vents toward a copse of trees. A small stream wandered through the trees. I have learned that where there are bushes and trees there is water. Streams offered an advantage to any campsite. We could still see the steam vents in the distance, but they had again merged into one large cloud rising into the sky. I wandered if the stream contained hot water. It didn't smell like spoiled duck eggs. I cupped my hands to quench my thirst. The water was cold and refreshing. I wondered how the two sources of water could be so close yet so different. There was much I did not understand about the land of boiling mud and spouting water.

"Takoda, why was there only steam coming from the vents? I had been told there would be gushing water." Takoda redirected my question to Wambleeska. I could have asked him directly, but I still found asking questions of such a distinguished Sioux chief intimidating.

"We are now in the sacred land of the spirit world," Wambleeska replied. "They are unpredictable. Sometimes they produced steam and other times they gush forth water higher than the tallest oak in your land of trees and lakes. Tomorrow Paytah will lead us to a vent that spouts water. The day is too short. We must camp here and leave early in the morning."

Chapter Twelve

"Cho-gan...Help me!"

I looked around. It was Takoda's voice, but I couldn't see him anywhere. I was standing alone in the tall grass. The cloudless sky was a beautiful azure-blue, and there was only the gentlest breeze, but the leaves on nearby trees were shaking violently. I looked beyond the trees at the tops of the hills; they were swaying back and forth as if their base were being shaken by an angry mythical dog or was it the ground beneath me that was shaking. I couldn't tell.

"Cho-gan...Help me!"

"Takoda, where are you," I asked. All I heard in reply was endless moaning. "Kanti, we must help Takoda." Kanti had been standing beside me, but now she was gone. "Kanti, where did you go? I can't see you."

"I'm helping Takoda," Kanti replied. The voice came from nowhere and everywhere all at the same time. Something strange was happening, something that simple logic could not explain. I couldn't see it, but I could feel

it. Both Takoda and Kanti were in danger, and I was helpless to do anything about it.

I awoke shaking and covered with sweat. My dreams had never been that intense. I still didn't understand the significance of the dreams, but a powerful spirit must be reaching out to me. Everyone was eating dried tatanka or packing supplies into backpacks as if nothing had happened. The hills were not waving. The air was quiet. The tree leaves were still. In the distance, I could see white columns rising from steam vents. No one showed any concern. It was a dream, but it felt so real.

I ate pemmican, preferring to save my dried tatanka until later. Then I drank my fill from the clear stream. Grandfather taught me to always drink my fill, as it is never known when the next opportunity will come.

"Paytah says we will see boiling mud and maybe some water spouts today," Takoda casually mentioned. He didn't seem concerned with his safety. I hadn't seen any rabbit holes. I didn't even know if rabbits lived in the land of purple hills. Perhaps Kanti and I had overreacted, but our trip did provide an opportunity to visit the land without trees and see the purple hills. I should relax and enjoy the adventure.

When everyone had eaten breakfast and packed their backpacks we set out walking west. Paytah said it would be a long day. The ground was no longer hot, so Kanti untied Whitefoot from his leash. I don't think Whitefoot liked the leash. He ran around sniffing here and there.

Paytah and Hassun lead us down a long valley. Short, stunted trees and large granite outcrops covered the hills forming the valley wall. Tall grass cloaked the valley floor. Several times we saw tatanka and antelope grazing in the distance. Trying to hunt them would have been time consuming and without guarantee of fruitful results. We had plenty of pemmican and dried meat.

Paytah and Hassun no longer scouted the trail. I assumed that meant there was little chance of getting lost. Maybe the boiling mud and spouting water was not far ahead of us. I gazed into the distance hoping to see spouting water, but all I saw was the bright sun in my eyes. Every once in a while I would catch a glimpse of a steam vent. I had seen too many of them to be impressed. We continued walking in silence as our eyes absorbed the many strange features of the land.

Around noon Paytah led us toward some rising steam near the west side of the valley. We had to climb a small hill to reach the steam vent. I wondered if this was worth the extra effort. We had seen so many steam vents.

When I crested the top of the mound I discovered the object of Paytah's quest. In front of us was a basin no more than two paces in diameter. It was filled with soft, moist mud. Every few moments a large gas bubble plowed its way to the surface. When it reached the top, the gas turned to that foul-smelling steam that we had encountered so many times before. The mud surrounding the bubble closed with a distinct "plop." There was something mesmerizing about the boiling mud, and we watched in silence. I don't think the mud was actually boiling but it did give the appearance of water boiling in slow motion. Paytah led us to a similar tub of mud one hundred paces away. When I looked around I saw four other plumes of steam. I had no doubt they were also mud pots. Anyone falling into the boiling mud would quickly die. I maintained my distance from the edge. Whitefoot seemed to understand this as he also kept his distance. No leash was needed.

One by one we retreated down the mound. The boiling mud was interesting, but like the steam vents, you can only watch them for so long. The vision of the bubbles boiling up through the mud was firmly lodged in my memory. It was another tale I could tell around future campfires—not that people would believe me.

"Paytah says we will camp for the evening at the far end of the valley," Wambleeska announced after everyone had gathered. "He wants to reach it before dark."

Paytah and Hassun headed off at a brisk pace quickly leaving the rest of us behind. Wambleeska and Grandfather couldn't walk that fast.

"Paytah and Hassun went ahead to gather firewood for the evening campfire," Takoda explained.

Now that Whitefoot was no longer on a leash, he wandered here and there to sniff this and that. Kanti lingered behind the others while Whitefoot finished exploring a helpless lizard. The lizard would run a short distance and stop. A nudge from Whitefoot's nose send it running again. Whitefoot considered it great sport; the lizard was not so sure. It was the opening I had been looking for. I wanted to talk to Kanti privately. I waited until the others were too far ahead of us to hear our conversation.

"Kanti, I need to talk to you," I whispered. She looked up at me with curiosity, but this quickly changed to concern when she saw my facial expression.

"You looked like you have just encountered one of the spirits from this spirit world."

"I feel like I have," I replied. "Last night I had another dream. The purple hills were waiving like tree leaves in a summer breeze just like before, but this time it felt real—not like a dream. Takoda was calling my name. You were beside me and then you were gone. I was helpless. I woke up thinking it was real, but you and Takoda were walking around is if nothing had happened."

We began walking again. We didn't want to get too far behind the others, although it was hard to get lost in the grassy meadow. Kanti didn't immediately reply to my confession, but I knew she was giving it serious thought.

"Chogan, I wasn't going to tell you this, because I didn't want to worry you, but I am also having bad dreams," Kanti finally replied. "The dreams are coming every night now. It's always that rabbit hole. I can hear Takoda pleading for help, but when I try to help him I get stuck in the hole. I always wake up before anything else happens. I've been searching for holes in the ground, but I all I found were those steam vents, and they're too small. That's why I haven't told you about the dreams. We can't protect Takoda from rabbit holes that don't exist."

"We need to catch up to the rest of them," I replied. "It's best we keep our dreams to ourselves until we know more."

Grandfather was looking back at us with concern, so we ran to catch up. Whitefoot was more than happy to run with us.

"We should stay together," Grandfather said. "This land has many unknowns and hidden dangers." It was as if Grandfather had overheard our conversation.

The rest of the day's journey passed without dangers. There were no more steam vents or boiling mud pots or large bears. The streams we crossed had clear, cool water. Tatanka and the occasional antelope took advantage of the deep grass—always at a distance.

Toward the end of the day I noticed smoke in the distance. I could now tell the difference between smoke and steam. Steam rose up and quickly evaporated into the air. Smoke continued upward and lingered in the air until gusts of wind blown the smoke away. What I was seeing reached high into the sky. There was more smoke than I would expect for a simple campfire. Paytah and Hassun must have added wet leaves to their fire to guide us toward the evening's campsite—it worked.

The campsite they had selected sat at the southern end of the valley. Large granite walls rose up on three sides. Three large oaks provided shelter from the morning dew. I say they were large, but they were still small compared to the tall oaks back home. I hadn't noticed it until our arrival, but there was a small steam vent no more than a hundred paces from our camping site.

"Those steam vents are everywhere," I said to no one in particular.

"That's not an ordinary steam vent," Wambleeska replied. He must have detected a bit of boredom in my voice. Three days ago I would have been excited upon seeing a steam vent, but after seeing so many steam vents the novelty wears thin. I looked up at Wambleeska hoping he would elaborate.

"What you see is a water spout. Water spouts spray water infrequently. If we are lucky it will do so while we are camped here. Most of the time there is little to see."

That added some excitement to the day. I had heard much about the spouting water. I didn't want to leave this enchanted land without seeing one.

"How often do they spout water?" Takoda asked. He likewise wanted to see a water spout before we returned to his village.

"There's no way to predict when the water will rise up from the earth. That's only known by those in the spirit world," Wambleeska replied. "It can be several full moons before some of the water spouts spill out their water. Others are more active. We can only wait and hope."

We sat under the oaks and ate our supper. I could have eaten some of my dried tatanka, but I prefer a warm meal when possible. I placed a chunk of pemmican on a stick and warmed it over the campfire. Pemmican can't be overheated or the rendered fat leaks out and much of the nourishment is lost. As soon as it began to drizzle into the fire I removed it and ate a very pleasant meal. We had walked a long distance and I was famished.

"I think the water spout is doing something," Takoda said.

I looked at the steam vent. It was indeed doing something, but I wasn't sure what. Mixed in with its steam were small spurts of water. We watched as we ate. Sometimes the water would spurt up more than waist high. I had seen springs where cool water bubbled up from the earth, but never more than a few finger breadths in height. The water display ceased for a moment or two and then resumed. The water rose up well above Grandfather's height. He could not have touched the top with the tips of his fingers. It was a wonderful display, and then it stopped. I assumed it was over. It was another strange event that few people would believe when I retold the tale to friends.

"Now I have seen all the wonders of this sacred place," I told Takoda.

I had barely finished my sentence when the water again gushed forth. Before one spurt ended, another began. Each one was taller than the one before until the water rose up higher than the mightiest oak back home. This cannot be I thought, but there it was before me. We watched in silence. Words would only ruin the spell. Then as quickly as it had begun it sputtered to a stop.

Wambleeska and Paytah had seen the water gush up from the ground in the past, but even they watched in awe. After the water ceased flowing, we sat around the campfire and quietly discussed the many wonders of this sacred land. We talked almost in a whisper, as if talking in a normal voice would be disrespectful of the spirit world. The water display repeated three more times before darkness forced us under our sleeping blankets. I fell asleep to the noise of yet another water display illuminated by starlight.

I awoke the following morning after another disturbing dream. I could tell by Kanti's somber mood that the spirit world also visited her during the night. Our dreams were always the same and offered no further guidance. There was never an ending. According to the Medicine Woman, our actions would dictate the ending for better or for worse. The outcome was always in doubt.

"Chogan, Kanti, I found the most interesting cave. You need to see it." Takoda had arisen before us and must have done some exploring. I was not surprised that this land had more to offer.

"How big is this cave?" I asked.

"It's a large cave," he replied. "I was able to enter standing upright. People have used the cave in the past for shelter. There are drawings on the walls."

Kanti and I once found a cave near where we lived. It also had evidence of prior use. Caves are interesting.

"Let me finish eating my dried tatanka, and then we can explore the cave together."

"People get lost in caves," Grandfather said. "We should go together. If it is a long cave, we will need torches."

What Grandfather said made sense, but I was in a hurry. I wanted to see the pictures on the wall. If the opening was as large as Takoda described there should be plenty of light. I quickly ate my dried tatanka and then waited until the others finished their breakfast.

After everyone finished eating, Takoda led an inquisitive group toward the southern end of the valley where large boulders replaced the grassy valley floor. A wall of granite extended high into the sky. I was hoping Takoda was not suggesting we climb to the top.

"It's over here." Takoda pointed to a dry river bed that wound its way toward the granite wall. Once we rounded some dense bushes, the opening to the cave became obvious. Water draining off the valley wall had carved a hole in the stone. The cave provided a large opening as Takoda had described. River-washed gravel covered the floor of the cave. Any boy my age would feel obligated to explore such a cave, although I would not want to be caught inside during a rain storm. I had no doubt a roaring river would quickly fill the opening. The morning light was shining into the entrance illuminating much of the cave, possibly all of it. I had no idea how far back the cave extended.

"There are the drawings," Takoda said. He pointed toward red marks high on the cave wall. Obviously, the water did not reach that high or it would have eroded away. One of the figures appeared to be a tatanka with an arrow protruding from its side.

"Grandfather, what is the meaning of these drawings?" Sometimes our people would paint symbols on canoes or other items. We always had the image of a flying eagle on our canoe, but these were multiple drawings. Someone had taken time to create them. Grandfather conversed briefly with Wambleeska in the Sioux language.

"It is probably tells the story of a hunter killing a tatanka," Grandfather replied. "We tell similar stories around our campfires."

I found several other drawings as I explored the cave. Most of them were near the mouth of the cave where light made the cave habitable. Takoda and I proceeded deeper into the cave, but without a torch there was little to see.

"Chogan, look at the size of that obsidian," Takoda bent down to give a tug on a large black rock embedded in the gravel floor. The rock budged, but did little more.

"You will never work it loose," I said. "If you did, it would be too heavy to carry back to your village." Obsidian made the sharpest knives and arrowheads. I could see why Takoda wanted it. It was a prized stone. We had no such stone in the land of trees and lakes.

"I'm heading back," I said. The others were leaving, and I was anxious to hear what new adventure was planned for the day. I had been in the cave a short time, but I had to squint my eyes as I left. My eyes were no longer used to the bright sun. I waited a moment or two until my eyes adjusted and then walked back to our campsite. The water spout was just finishing one of its displays. I don't think I could ever get bored watching the water shoot up into the air.

"What are we doing today?" I asked Grandfather, but he was not listening—at least not to me. Wambleeska was also acting strange.

"Grandfather, is something wrong?"

"What do you hear, Chogan?

I listened for a few moments. "I hear nothing," I replied.

"That is the point," Grandfather said. "There are no birds singing their songs in the trees. The crickets are no longer chirping. No birds are flying in the sky."

I listened again. Grandfather was right. There was no sound at all. Nature is never quiet. There is always some creature that wants to make its presence known. I waited in silence. Then a deep rumble filled the air. The ground began to shake. I looked up and the purple mountains were swaying like leaves during a summer breeze. It was just like my dreams.

"EVERYONE, MOVE AWAY FROM THE VALLEY WALLS," Grandfather yelled.

The reason for his concern was obvious. Large boulders were rolling down from their previous perches high up on the valley wall. Any one of them could quickly kill a person. I ran with the others toward the center of the valley. No one stopped running until we were more than two hundred paces from the valley wall. I stopped and looked back. The canyon walls were still crumbling even though the ground no longer shook.

"What happened?" I asked. I wasn't expecting an answer, but I had to ask. I assumed no one would know.

"I have felt the earth move once before," Wambleeska replied. "When one occurs there are frequently more. Something has disturbed the spirit world. We must leave this place immediately."

As if to confirm his point, the ground again shook, but not as violently as before. Rocks were no longer falling from the walls. Birds were again flying in the air. Nature returned to its normal noisy self.

"I think we can safely return for our backpacks and sleeping gear," Wambleeska said. "If you feel the ground move again—run."

We returned to the camp site next to the water spout. It was again gushing fourth as if the ground had not moved. I rolled up my moose skin and tied it to my back pack. All the while I watched the boulders clinging to the valley wall. If any one of them so much as quivered I planned to drop everything and run.

"Where is Takoda?" Kanti asked.

I looked up. He was nowhere to be seen. I couldn't remember if he ran with us when we ran away from the falling rocks. He could have been hit by a rock before he had time to get away.

"TAKODA! TAKODA!" There was more urgency in Wambleeska's voice each time he called out his grandson's name.

"Who saw Takoda last?" Grandfather asked. Everyone looked at everyone else, waiting for a reply.

"The last time I saw him he was in the cave trying to pry loose a piece of obsidian that was embedded in the gravel," I said. "I am sure he followed us out soon after that." But I wasn't sure. I couldn't remember seeing him leave the cave.

Chapter Thirteen

Wambleeska dropped his walking stick and raced toward the cave entrance, ignoring arthritic knees that previously hindered movement. Takoda couldn't be in the cave, but I could find no other explanation for his absence. We arrived at the massive granite wall and stared up in silence, wishing for a miracle that could not be granted. The wall of stone extended upward almost vertically. A large pile of rock and dirt at the base of the valley wall confirmed a recent landslide. Several large boulders still hung from unstable perches, where further tremors could send them rolling down upon us. They should have filled me with fear, but they didn't. I searched the debris looking for the cave entrance; it was hardly recognizable. The entire roof of the cave had collapsed reducing it to a pile of rubble. If Takoda were lying under those rocks, he could not have survived.

We carefully inspected the pile of stone and debris that moments before had been a cave. How could this be? I looked up at Wambleeska, hoping for an answer or at least some encouragement, but no words of wisdom or encouragement were forthcoming. Tears dripped down his cheeks. He made no effort to brush them away. I didn't think a mighty chief of the Sioux Nation was capable of crying, but he was crying without shame.

"He was the only son of my only daughter," he said. Wambleeska then looked toward Kanti and me. You came a long distance to warn us of a hole in the ground. I did not heed your warnings. I should not have let Takoda enter the cave. It is my fault and mine alone that he has left us for the spirit world."

"NO, NO, THIS ISN'T RIGHT!

I had never heard Kanti yell at her elders. She was strong willed, but she still had respect for the wisdom of people with advanced years. Her dreams had affected her emotionally more than I had realized.

"The cave was as tall as a grown man," Kanti explained in a much more subdued voice. "Grandfather would have found it difficult to touch the roof with his hands. The hole in my dreams was not much larger than a rabbit hole. I barely fit into it. I even got stuck. There is no way I could have gotten stuck in this cave. It is all wrong."

"Kanti, your dreams carried hidden meanings that we did not fully understand," Grandfather said, "but dreams are not real life. Sometimes they are not totally correct."

The ground shook again, but unlike the first tremor only a few pebbles fell from their elevated locations. It still made me nervous. I was ready to run if any stone larger than my fist were to fall.

"Do you want us to remove the stones to see if we can recover the body?" Grandfather looked at Wambleeska. It was his land. It was his grandson. He should be the one to make that decision.

"One person has died, but six people still live. This is sacred ground. There is no more beautiful or fitting place for Takoda to rest forever. No, we must ensure that those who still live return safely to their villages. We must leave at once."

I could see that Kanti wanted to protest, but wisdom finally got the better of her emotions. We traveled most of the summer to warn Takoda of the danger. We failed. There was nothing more we could do. We had done our best and there should be no shame. I began to follow the others back to our camp site where our backpacks awaited us. It would be a long trip home.

"Come here, Whitefoot." Kanti waited for Whitefoot.

Whitefoot normally followed Kanti everywhere, but he was an inquisitive dog. He needed to sniff and explore anything that appeared new. In this land that was everything. But he also needed to be in the lead, well in front of our group. It was surprising that Kanti would have to call him. I looked back to see what had captured Whitefoot's fascination. He was scratching and sniffing at a large rock near the cave entrance.

"Whitefoot, come here."

He again ignored Kanti's command. Whitefoot now had everyone's attention. We couldn't leave without him, but we also couldn't remain at the base of the valley wall where more boulders could come rolling down at any moment. The boulder that had Whitefoot's interest was too large for me to move. The way Whitefoot was acting, I feared moving the rock would reveal Takoda's crushed body. It created a vivid image in my mind. I did not want to add reality to that image. Hassun and Paytah's thoughts mirrored mine; however, they had more courage. It was a large boulder, but Hassun and Paytah were able to wrestle it to the side after much effort.

I was relieved to discover no crushed body parts. There was nothing beneath the boulder other than the stones and gravel from the dry river bed. Whitefoot was not satisfied. He continued sniffing the ground and then poked his head into a small opening under an arch of stone. Whitefoot decided he did not fit and retreated.

"It's the rabbit hole. Just like my dreams!"

It was indeed a cavity not much bigger that a rabbit hole, but still just a cavity. I assumed I could touch the back wall of the hole if I were to try. It changed nothing. We needed to leave before more rocks fell down the valley wall.

"I'm going to crawl inside," Kanti said. "If my dream is correct, I'll find Takoda."

"You'll never fit in that tiny hole," I told her. Kanti was built like a lodge pole. I didn't know how she stayed so skinny with her voracious appetite, but there was no way she would fit inside that hole.

"I've done it many times. I'll fit."

Kanti couldn't separate her dreams from reality. What occurred in a dream was only a dream. There was no way I could persuade her otherwise with logic. She had to discover this for herself. Kanti lay flat against the rocks of the stream bed and inserted her head in the hole. With a bit of wiggling she was able to squeeze her shoulders into the hole.

"Kanti, that's far enough." I wasn't sure if she could hear me. Only her legs protruded from the hole.

"Grandfather, we must stop her." I looked to Grandfather for help.

"The spirit world reached out to Kanti causing her to walk a great distance to save a friend. I do not understand the wishes of the spirit world—only Kanti does. We must let her continue her quest. We must not interfere even though what she is doing presents grave danger. I am hoping the spirit world that brought her here will watch over her."

I wish I had that much faith in the spirit world. If they wanted to be helpful they would have prevented Takoda from entering the cave. I bend down to look into the hole; I could no longer see Kanti. I dug away at the loose rocks and gravel of the riverbed. I stuck my head into the enlarge hole and called out to Kanti. I heard a faint garbled reply. She was still alive somewhere under that pile of rocks. I scooped out more rocks and gravel.

I feared removing rocks from above as that might cause the roof to collapse, but digging rocks from the riverbed was probably safe. I reached out with both arms and scooped up the loose grave. After several scoops I was able to insert my entire torso, but it was difficult dragging gravel back to the opening.

"I need my moose skin," I said. I unrolled my bedroll. No one questioned my wisdom—except me. Takoda was most surely dead, Kanti was crawling under a mountain, and I was crawling after her. Where is the wisdom in that?

I pushed the moose skin in front of me and covered it with stones and debris from the riverbed; then I dragged it out of the hole. I found that to be more efficient. My stomach was pinched against the riverbed and my back was scrapping the roof of the tunnel, but I was moving forward. Even my feet were now within the hole.

"Kanti, can you hear me? We need to get out of here."

I heard another muffled reply that I couldn't understand. She remained a significant distance in front of me. I was surprised the tunnel extended that far. Whatever distance we crawled had to be repeated backwards to escape this tunnel. Crawling backward would not be easy. I reached forward; there was no wall. I crawled into the opening. Further exploring revealed a small pocket within the rock. I feared it was the end of the tunnel as all I could feel was the stone wall. I was in total darkness. Even during a moonless night there are stars to provide a meager light. This darkness was like nothing I had ever seen.

"Kanti, can you hear me?"

Again there was an unintelligent reply. She was facing forward and her replies didn't travel well toward those behind her. It did provide a direction. I slid my hands down the wall toward where I had heard Kanti's voice and discovered a small opening. It had to be the continuation of the tunnel. I was pleased to discover I fit without further excavation. If I did have to remove more rocks I wouldn't have to take them back to the tunnel opening. I could stash them in this pocket.

I crawled forward. It was much easier now that I did not have to remove rocks in my way. My back still scrapped the roof of the tunnel. The ground again began to shake. I covered my head with my hands as if that would protect me if the tunnel were to collapse. Sand and gravel fell on my neck, but the tremor was nothing like the big one we had felt earlier. There was no guarantee that larger tremors would not shake the mountain. I continued crawling forward.

"Kanti, are you still there?"

"I'm stuck, just like my dreams. There's a huge rock in my way."

"Can you crawl backward? We need to get out of here. Kanti, this is too dangerous."

She sounded much closer. The rock blocked her advance, allowing me to catch up. Maybe now I could talk her out of this endeavor. I must admit, I was scared. The stone blocking her way was always the end of her dream. Her dreams would no longer provide guidance. We needed to leave the tunnel before the earth trembled again.

"We can't give up now," Kanti replied. "I can hear Takoda on the other side of this stone. I'm sure it's him. It is just like my dream. He's asking for help."

Sometimes Kanti's imagination gets the best of her. It wouldn't surprise me if this was one of those times. The entire cave seemed to have collapsed. Takoda was a good friend, but he was most likely dead. It would benefit no one if Kanti and I were also to die.

"I can push the rock forward," Kanti said. "Maybe I can roll in front of me until I find an opening."

I continued crawling forward. If the Medicine Woman was correct, anything beyond that stone was uncharted territory. We were creating our own future. We now controlled our own destiny—assuming there were no more large tremors. The tremors still sent shivers down my spine even though they were small. A big tremor could occur without warning.

"I'm inside the cave. Takoda's alive!"

I wasn't sure what "inside the cave" meant. I thought I was well inside the cave, but I didn't find that worth bragging about. My stomach was resting on the riverbed and my back was scraping the top of the tunnel. I had seen little improvement in the quality of the tunnel since I entered, but the fact that Takoda was alive was music to my ears. I couldn't see how he could have survived the avalanche of rock and stone falling from the cave ceiling. I was now close enough to hear Takoda and Kanti talking. Takoda's survival was more than Kanti's fantasy.

I inched my way forward. I knew I was getting close to Kanti and Takoda. Their voices were no longer muffled. I reached out, but the tunnel wall was gone as was the ceiling. I had entered another pocket. I pulled myself into the opening. It was much larger than the previous pocket I crawled through. I climbed to my knees and then to my feet. I still couldn't touch the ceiling.

"Kanti, where are you?" Kanti's reply made it sound like she was standing beside me, but all I could see was darkness. I could touch my finger to my eye and never see it. Even though I was no longer confined to the small tunnel, I would be lying if I said I wasn't scared.

"Chogan, we're inside the cave," Kanti said. "This section of the cave didn't collapse."

I reached out to touch Kanti, but she was nowhere within reach. Caves can do strange things with sound. She could be anywhere. I was afraid to walk in the dark for fear of tripping over a stone. I slowly shuffled my feet forward until my feet hit a solid object. A scream of pain confirmed the solid object was Takoda. Much as I wanted to hear Takoda's voice, I didn't wish to inflict pain.

"We're down here," Kanti said. "Down by the ground."

"Go easy on my left arm," Takoda said. "I think it's broken."

I bent down and slowly probed with my hands until I found Takoda's feet. From his orientation, I had no doubt I kicked his broken arm. Then I reached over Takoda until I felt Kanti. She was kneeling on the uninjured side.

"How'd you guys get in here?" Takoda asked. "I looked all over for a way out. I assumed I would die in here."

"Kanti found a small tunnel. It was just like her dreams. I had to enlarge it before I would fit. We're the same size. If I can make it through the tunnel, you should be able to squeeze through."

I heard Takoda let out an audible sigh. I assumed be would be overjoyed about leaving the cave. Before we arrived, he was facing assured death.

"There is no way I can crawl through the tunnel with a broken arm," Takoda said. "I appreciate what you did. It was very risky, but you need to save yourselves. One more large tremor and this cave will collapse."

"Chogan, what are we going to do? We can't leave Takoda, not after we came so far. The Medicine Woman said the future was up to us."

It was pitch black, but I could feel Kanti's eyes glaring at me. I knew her hands were resting on her hips. It was her classic "Chogan, do something" stance. It was Kanti who decided to run off with the Winnebago merchants. When I caught up with her, it was Kanti who insisted we travel to the purple hills to save Takoda. Now that a solution to our problem was impossible, I was in charge. It had taken all my energy to reach the inside of the cave. I questioned if I had remaining energy to crawl back out of the cave. Takoda was right; there was no way he could crawl through that small tunnel with a broken arm. The full moon would come and go before we could remove the rocks that filled the cave. The way the ground was shaking, it was likely new rocks could replace the rocks as fast as we removed them.

"Well, what are we going to do?"

Chapter Fourteen

"I'm thinking," I responded.

"What the two of you are going to do is crawl back out of this cave," Takoda said. "Please tell my grandfather that this was not his fault."

What Takoda was saying made logical sense, not that Kanti could understand logic. I should send her back while Takoda and I considered possible solutions, but if Kanti had come this far it was unlikely she would leave.

"Do you have any injuries other than your broken arm?" The extent of his injuries could influence our options. Crawling through the tunnel was already eliminated by his broken arm.

"I think I have a cut on my head from a falling rock, but no other injuries besides my broken arm. I had just worked loose that large piece of obsidian when the roof began to fall on me. I should have left without the obsidian as you suggested. It's too big to carry back to the village."

"I'm going to start removing rocks from the opening."

Removing rocks from the entrance was like empting Gitche Gumee with a small cup, but Kanti needed something to do. She was never one to wait. I couldn't see Kanti, but I could hear her shuffle around Takoda. Then I heard her fall. The dry riverbed was mostly flat, but there were a few rocks that had fallen when the ground shook. I assumed she had tripped over one of them.

"WHAT IS THIS?"

I could tell by the tone of her voice that she wasn't injured, but she was definitely angry. She should have known the cave floor was littered with rocks.

"I tripped over some sort of animal skin. What's that doing here?"

"That's my sleeping blanket," I replied.

"You were planning to spend the night?" I'm the one who normally uses sarcasm, but Kanti was angry. She needed to vent her anger.

"I used it to drag rocks from the tunnel. I'm not as skinny as you." I was not sure if that answer pacified Kanti. She can be quick tempered, but she soon forgets. It did give me an idea.

"Takoda, how much pain can you tolerate?"

"If pain is optional, I would prefer to do without it, but I don't think I have a choice."

"There is a way we can get you out of here, but it will be painful."

"If you have a way to get me out of here, I will tolerate any amount of pain," Takoda replied, "as long as you can ignore my screaming."

I knew the last part was said in jest, but what I was planning would be very painful. I wondered if he would be up to it. At the moment I saw no other way of removing him from the cave.

"I have the moose-skin I use for sleeping. It is longer than you are tall. If we get you on it, I can drag you through the tunnel just as I did the stones."

I waited for what I said to sink in. His broken arm would surely scrap against the wall. There was no way I could protect him. It was a long tunnel with many curves and bends. But if we didn't do something soon, more rocks could fall. All three of us could die. Leaving him to die alone seemed out of the question.

"You have two choices," Takoda replied. "Either you drag me out of here kicking and screaming or the two of you leave without me. Either way, the two of you need to get out of this cave now."

"We'll try to be gentle."

I grabbed the moose skin and crawled to Takoda's left side. I unrolled it until it stretched from Takoda's head to his feet. I then slowly lifted his broken arm. I could feel the broken ends grinding together. He needed to have the broken bone splinted but there was nothing in the cave we could use for a splint.

"Grab your wrist with your good hand," I said. "That should immobilize the bone somewhat. We need to roll you onto your right side."

Takoda grabbed his wrist and I gradually rolled him away from the moose skin. Then I eased him back onto the moose skin. If it had been I, I would have screamed in pain, but Takoda was bearing it well. He was still not centered. We needed to move him. That would create more pain.

"Takoda, we need to move you toward your left. Keep hanging on to your wrist. That should reduce the pain. I will lift your shoulders and, Kanti, I want you to move his legs.

I positioned myself near Takoda's head and slipped my hands under his shoulders. We didn't need to move him far, but he did need to be centered on the moose skin.

"We'll move him on the count of three. One. Two. Three."

I lifted Takoda's shoulders and moved him over as gently as I could. I assumed Kanti was doing the same with the legs. I straddled Takoda and shuffled toward his legs. His shoulders and legs were in good position but his hips bent at an angle. That part of Takoda's body had not moved. I lifted Takoda's hips and straightened his body. I could feel Takoda flinch each time I moved him. Dragging him through the tunnel would not be pleasant.

"Is everyone ready?" I asked.

"Do it," Takoda responded.

I heard no comment from Kanti. I assumed that meant she was ready. I grabbed a small segment of the moose skin near Takoda's head. Dragging Takoda through the tunnel would be fatiguing. It didn't occur to me until I was ready that I didn't know where the tunnel was. It was not like I could see it in the dark. Takoda had been my only landmark and we had moved him.

I crawled to one of the sides and skimmed my hands over the wall. I couldn't find the opening. My worst fears had come true. The last tremor must have closed the opening.

"I can't find the tunnel," I said.

"I'll help you," Kanti replied. "It's not very big and it's down low."

That much I already knew. We both patted at the walls looking for any kind of opening. If rocks hadn't closed the opening, it shouldn't be that hard to find, but we couldn't find it.

"Found it!"

"Stay where you are. I'm crawling toward you. Keep talking."

That was a relief. I began crawling toward Kanti's voice. When I reached her she took my hand and directed me to a small hole in the wall of rock. It was so small. It was hard to believe I had just squeezed through that hole. Now I had to find Takoda.

"Takoda, talk to me."

I place a foot inside the hole and stretched out toward Takoda's voice. I couldn't quite reach him, but I now knew the orientation between Takoda and the hole. I crawled back to Takoda and again took a firm grip on the moose skin.

"You ready?" I asked.

"Let's get out of here."

I pulled the moose skin toward the tunnel. Takoda was heavier than I thought. When I reached the wall, I felt around with my foot until it found the tunnel opening. Pulling Takoda across the dry river bed inside the cave would be easy compared with the tunnel. I was beginning to wonder if it was possible.

"Kanti, make sure Takoda's legs stay on the moose skin."

"Will it help if I push on his feet?"

If Takoda stiffened his body, pushing on his feet might help, but I wondered how much force Kanti could apply once we were inside the tunnel.

"We'll see how well this works first," I replied.

I slithered my legs into the tunnel and then tried to pull Takoda toward me. Instead of Takoda coming toward me, I pulled myself out of the tunnel. My plan was a failure. There was no backup plan.

"This isn't working," I said. "Instead of pulling Takoda toward me, I pulled myself toward him."

"Is there any way you can anchor your feet?" Takoda asked.

"Let me try it again."

I wiggled my feet back into the hole and pressed them against the sides. This time I was able to pull Takoda toward me. I wiggled farther into the tunnel until my legs were inside. That made it much easier to anchor myself. I gave another pull. We were making progress. When I was entirely inside the tunnel except for my head and hands I paused to ensure Takoda was lined up appropriately. I didn't want to press his broken arm against the opening.

"Okay, Takoda, we are entering the tunnel. Hold on tightly to the wrist of your broken arm."

I heard a low grunt from Takoda. He would experience pain; there was no way I could avoid that. I tried to push those thoughts from my mind and focus on getting us out from underneath all that rock.

Crawling through the tunnel backwards was not an easy endeavor. Pushing with my hands didn't help. I had to wiggle my body backward. It was a long tunnel. Crawling backward through the entire tunnel would be time-consuming. I just hoped the on and off tremors had not blocked the tunnel. I grabbed ahold of the moose skin and gave it another pull. Takoda gradually followed behind me.

"Takoda, let me know when you need a break. Kanti, are you doing Okay?"

"Go ahead and get it over with," Takoda replied. I could tell he was gritting his teeth.

"I'm inside the tunnel now," Kanti said, "but I'm having trouble keeping Takoda's feet on the moose skin."

"Let me know whenever either of you needs to pause."

I paused until Kanti gave me the go-ahead. If truth were told, I was the one who needed a break. My fingers were beginning to ache. It was difficult getting a firm grip on the moose skin. I rolled the edge of the skin until I could wrap my fingers around it. I inched my way backward and gave a pull. That worked better.

At least the three of us could talk to each other. I'm not saying I am afraid of the dark or confined spaces, but I think I would go raving mad if I were alone with no emotional support from Takoda or Kanti. I wondered if they were also scared. If they were, they were hiding it well.

I continued pulling Takoda through the tunnel with frequent stops to rest my hands and arms. The sharp edges of the freshly cracked rock cut into my forearms. I was sure any light would confirm many deep cuts and scratches. They would heal with time. The aching pain in my forearms was harder to ignore.

"Hold up. Takoda's feet are slipping off the moose skin again."

I waited for Kanti to adjust Takoda's feet. I could adjust Takoda's head and shoulders and she could adjust his feet, but if Takoda's hips were to slide off the moose skin, there was no way to reposition him on the skin, not in the cramped tunnel.

I now regretted not sending Kanti out first, not that she would have listened to me. If Takoda should get stuck or I was no longer able to pull him forward, Kanti would be doomed. There was no way she could pull Takoda back out of the tunnel, not at her weight. And there was no way she could get around him. He was blocking the tunnel.

I finally reached the enlarged cavity. That was about the half way point. At least we were making progress. I wondered if Kanti could work her way around Takoda and get in front of me, but I needed her where she was. I needed Kanti to keep Takoda's feet squarely on the skin. I wiggled backward and pulled Takoda toward me. It might have been my imagination, but I thought I was beginning to see dark shadows. Total darkness can do strange things to the mind.

"I'm not sure, but I think I can see some light." I didn't know if I said that to cheer up Takoda and Kanti or to cheer me. We all needed some hope.

"Lay as flat as you can," Kanti said.

I wasn't sure what Kanti had in mind, but it was a good excuse to wrest my muscles. I did as she asked.

"I can see dim light behind you," Kanti said. "We still have a ways to go, but that light sure looks pretty."

Kanti's observation gave me new energy. I wiggled backward and pulled, wiggled backward and pulled. The dark shadow turned into Takoda. I could see his head and shoulders. I could hear voices that that didn't belong to Takoda or Kanti. I wiggled backward and pulled, wiggled backward and pulled. Someone grabbed my ankles. My abdomen scraped across the dry river bed. I could no longer hang on to the moose skin. I had to let go. Hassun reached into the hole and grabbed the skin.

"Be gentle," I said. "Takoda has a broken arm."

I didn't know if Hassun heard me, but Takoda was not complaining. He was happy to see sunlight when Hassun pulled him into the open. I'm sure Takoda thought he would never see the sun again. Kanti effortlessly crawled out of the hole by herself. I don't know where she gets her energy.

"Let's get him away from the rocks." Wambleeska grabbed a corner of my moose skin. Paytah, Hassun, and Grandfather did likewise. I wouldn't say they ran, but it was a very fast walk as they carried Takoda back to our campsite by the gushing water. Kanti and I squinted our eyes and followed after them. The bright sunlight was almost painful after spending time in total darkness.

Kanti and I sat in the shade of an oak tree while Wambleeska and Grandfather crafted a splint and sling for Takoda. He seemed to be in less pain now that the arm was splinted. He could sit up on the ground.

"I'm sorry I placed you in such danger," he said. "I wanted that obsidian rock so badly. I guess it will stay hidden in that cave forever."

"Look between your feet," Kanti said. "I placed the rock on the moose skin before we left."

"No wonder you were so difficult to drag. I am glad you didn't choose a heavier rock."

I walked over and picked up the stone. It was a beautiful piece of obsidian. It could make many knives and spear points, but it was too heavy to carry back to the village.

"You'll never carry this back to your village," I said. "It's too heavy."

"Break it in half with another large stone."

I found a large irregularly shaped granite stone. It must have rolled down from the hills when the earth shook. I lifted it up and then hammered down on the obsidian rock as Takoda had requested. The rock split into three pieces with sharp, jagged edges. That was what made obsidian so valuable. Takoda took the two largest pieces and gave them to Kanti and me.

"You have saved my life not once, but twice. You are true friends. I will never forget you. This obsidian should be small enough to carry, but still valuable when you return to your village. I wish there was more I could do to thank you."

"I also need to thank you," Wambleeska said with tears in his eyes. "Takoda is the only son of my only daughter. You traveled a long distance and endured many hardships. You risked your lives, but you brought my grandson back from the dead. You have displayed great courage and wisdom for being so young. You and your family will always find a welcome home in my teepee. When you wish to return home, I will have men of the village escort you to the land of the river people. My men will bring many skins, hand-crafted jewelry, and obsidian to trade for wooden canoes. There will be excess merchandise to carry home. If you are lucky, you will catch the Winnebago merchants before they return to your land."

Wambleeska was right. We had traveled a long distance, motivated only by the sincerity of Kanti's dreams. But the many hardships we had endured would become tales to tell around campfires. I had always wanted to travel to the land with no trees. I wanted to see those shaggy deer. I wanted to see the purple hills that rose up to kiss the sky. I had seen all that and more. I had also seen the boiling pots of mud and the water that spouts high into the air. It was very beautiful, but I missed the lakes and streams. I missed the forest of tall oaks and maples the continued forever. The land with no trees was an interesting place to visit, but it was time to go home.

SUPPORT INDIE AUTHORS

If you enjoyed this novel, please find the book on Amazon.com and leave a review with plenty of stars. You don't need to purchase the book on Amazon to leave a comment. The comment only requires a line or two. Example: "Name of novel" is well written with an engaging plot. I would highly recommend reading "name of novel."

Native American Series

Chogan and the Winnebego Merchant is the fourth novel in the Chogan Native American series. If you enjoy *Chogan and the Winnebego Merchant* you will probably enjoy *Chogan and the Gray Wolf, Chogan and the White Feather, and Chogan and the Sioux Warrior.*

Chogan and the Gray Wolf
(Book #1 in the Chogan Native American Series)

It is 100 years B.C. (Before Columbus), and life is good for twelve-year-old Chogan and his ten-year-old sister until a Grizzly Bear terrorizes their Indian village along the southern shore of Lake Superior. The bear crushes wigwams with its massive weight and destroys precious strips of meat women had hung on racks to dry. Despite the danger, life must go on if Chogan and his family are to survive. Chogan and his sister venture into the forest of virgin white pine to check their snares and discover an orphaned wolf pup. The bear has killed the wolf pup's mother, and has left the pup to die.

Chogan adopts the young wolf knowing he must return the wolf to the wild at the end of the summer. Under Chogan's care, the wolf pup survives and grows to adulthood. The time comes when Chogan and the wolf must part and go their separate ways. The wolf quickly adapts to the wild but never forgets his friend. Chogan had saved the pup's life, and fate will soon provide the wolf with a chance to return the favor.

Chogan and the White Feather

(Book #2 in the Chogan Native American Series)

Life along the southern shore of Lake Superior would be pleasant, if not for the village bully, and every Indian village had one. Unfortunately, twelve-year-old Chogan and his ten-year-old sister Kanti have the misfortune of residing in a village with two bullies. But size isn't everything, and Chogan and Kanti's devious tactics usually gets the best of Ahanu and Tarragon. That all changes when Kanti unwittingly bets her prized spear against Ahanu's bear-claw necklace. If Kanti is to win the wager and reclaim her spear, she will need the assistance of Mishosha (the Magician of the Lake) and Gitche Migizi (an eagle so large men can ride on its back).

Life becomes even more difficult when Chogan and Kanti come face-to-face with the Windigo—a stretch of river so treacherous villagers named it after a mythical beast that devours human flesh. During a full moon the wailing of a thousand souls can be heard within Windigo's mournful roar. If Chogan and Kanti are not careful, their voices will be added to that number.

Chogan and the Sioux Warrior

(Book #3 in the Chogan Native American Series)

Life is peaceful for twelve-year-old Chogan and his ten-year-old sister, Kanti, until Sioux warriors attack their village along the southern shore of Gitche Gumee. The raiders escape by canoe—all except for one warrior who retreats into the woods with an arrow embedded in his thigh.

While checking his snares, Chogan stumbles upon the missing warrior only to discover the warrior is Takoda—a mere boy no older than Chogan. With Kanti's help Chogan removes the arrow from Takoda's thigh, saving his life. Now Chogan and Kanti must conceal Takoda's presence from the angry villagers who seek revenge.

To complicate Chogan's already complicated life, a traveling Winnebago merchant discovers the returning Sioux warriors have lied to their people. They claim they were victims of an Ojibway ambush, and that the Ojibway captured and tortured Takoda. Takoda's grandfather, who is chief of the Sioux, is now preparing to avenge his grandson's death.

If Chogan and Kanti are to prevent certain war between two mighty Indian nations, they must deliver Takoda to his grandfather. They must paddle half way across Gitche Gumee in the dead of night while evading Sioux and Ojibway scouts (both of whom might kill them if captured) and then return Takoda to his grandfather. Their only assistance comes from the Gitche Manitou who provides a brilliant display of Northern Lights (waasanoode) to guide their way.

Below are the web pages that accompanied *Chogan and the Winnebago Merchant*. Copy and past the underlined sections into your computer's search engine to view the web pages.

Winnebago-Merchant.com/skyhunters.htm This web site describes Legend of Moosebird, Chickadee & Robin.

The-Sioux-Warrior.com/pemmican/index.html If you don't remember what pemmican is or how it is made, you may want to review Chogan's website from Chogan and the Sioux Warrior

Winnebago-Merchant.com/travois.htm This web site further describes (with photos) the travois used by the Winnebago merchants.

Winnebago-Merchant.com/buffalo.htm To learn more about tatanka check out Chogan's buffalo web site.

Winnebago-Merchant.com/Mandan.htm *The Mandan were river people with villages along the Missouri River. You can read more about them at Chogan's Mandan web site.*

Web pages from Chogan and the Gray Wolf

Some of you may have missed reading the first book in the Chogan series. If so, below are some of the web pages that accompanied that novel. Copy the underlined section into your computer's search engine to view the web page.

www.The-Gray-Wolf.com/baggataway/ This web page describes the Indian game of baggataway, which we now call lacrosse. There are also pictures of Fort Michilimackinac where a game of baggataway turned into a massacre during the Pontiac rebellion.

www.The-Gray-Wolf.com/snares/ This web page shows how Chogan made the snares he uses to catch small game.

www.The-Gray-Wolf.com/wapatoo/ Wapatoo (also known as arrowhead) is an edible plant. This web page shows how to identify the plant and cook the tubers.

www.The-Gray-Wolf.com/copper/ Thousands of years ago an ancient race of people mined copper in Michigan's Upper Peninsula. This web page shows the types of copper they mined and well as a typical mine.

www.The-Gray-Wolf.com/cord/ This web page shows how to make string and rope out of milkweed fiber.

www.The-Gray-Wolf.com/fire./ Need to start a fire without matches? This web site will show you how Chogan starts a fire with a spindle and fireboard.

www.The-Gray-Wolf.com/manoomin/ Manoomin, also known as wild rice, was a major food source for Chogan and his family. This web site shows how manoomin was harvested and processed.

Web pages from Chogan and the White Feather

In case you missed Chogan's web pages while reading *Chogan and the White Feather*, below is a list and description of the five web pages. Copy the underlined section into your computer's search engine to view the web page.

www.The-White-Feather.com/wigwam/ Describes how wigwams are made with interior and exterior pictures of a completed wigwam.

www.The-White-Feather.com/acorns/ Describes how to pick the best acorns and how to prepare them for consumption. The web page concludes with a recipe for acorn cookies.

www.The-White-Feather.com/totem/ Describes the Ojibway clan system and provides examples of the original five totems. Also explains the difference between a totem and a manitou.

www.The-White-Feather.com/canoe/ Provides a picture showing a short canoe under construction and explains the difference between a short utility canoe like Chogan's and the larger cargo canoes.

www.The-White-Feather.com/spear/ Provides a description with pictures on how to make a spear similar to Kanti's spear.

Web pages from Chogan and the Sioux Warrior

In case you missed Chogan's web pages while reading *Chogan and the Sioux Warrior*, below is a list and description of the six web pages. Copy the underlined section into your computer's search engine to view the web page.

www.The-Sioux-Warrior.com/pemmican/ Describes how to make pemmican from strips of meat and animal fat. Pemmican was the Indian equivalent of today's trail mix.

www.The-Sioux-Warrior.com/languages/ Describes the three basic language groups used by the Indians in the north-central and north-east United States.

www.The-Sioux-Warrior.com/torches/ Shows how Ojibway Indians made torches from birch bark.

www.The-Sioux-Warrior.com/northernlights/ Provides pictures of northern lights and explains the Indian folklore and scientific explanations for northern lights.

www.The-Sioux-Warrior.com/rocktripe/ Provides instructions in the preparation of rock tripe with photographs.

www.The-Sioux-Warrior.com/rocks/ Describes valuable stones such as catlinite and obsidian.

ABOUT THE AUTHOR

Larry Buege is an award-winning author who has always been fascinated by pre-Columbian Native Americans. He currently lives along the southern shore of Lake Superior, which is the setting for his Native American Series.